"Still Running Away?" Zachary Drawled.

The cruel thrust of his words was nearly lost in the soft inflection of his tone.

"I didn't run away from you, Zachary," Christen retorted, her hackles rising as always when he baited her.

"Didn't you?"

"I made a choice."

"*After* you climbed out of my bed." His voice dropped to a guttural jeer. "What happened, Christen? Were you afraid you couldn't be woman enough for me?" A gasp hissed through her teeth as the barb found its mark. "Ahh," he murmured. "From that little reaction, should I assume that after five years, I've stumbled on the truth?"

"Stop it! You're giving a casual encounter more importance than it merits."

"Is that all it was for you?" Zachary asked almost too softly to be heard.

"Yes!" She spun away, turning from him, afraid that even in the darkness he would read the truth on her face....

Dear Reader:

Welcome to the world of Silhouette Desire. Join me as we travel to a land of incredible passion and tantalizing romance—a place where dreams can, and do, come true.

When I read a Silhouette Desire, I sometimes feel as if I'm going on a little vacation. I can relax, put my feet up, and be transported to a new world...a world that has, naturally, a perfect hero just waiting to whisk me away! These are stories to remember, containing moments to treasure.

Silhouette Desire novels are romantic love stories— sensuous yet emotional. As a reader, you not only see the hero and heroine fall in love, you also feel what they're feeling.

Look for books by some of your favorite Silhouette Desire authors: Joan Hohl, BJ James, Linda Lael Miller and Diana Palmer.

So enjoy!

Lucia Macro
Senior Editor

BJ JAMES

WINTER MORNING

SILHOUETTE *Desire*

Published by Silhouette Books New York
America's Publisher of Contemporary Romance

SILHOUETTE BOOKS
300 East 42nd St., New York, N.Y. 10017

ISBN: 0-373-05595-1

First Silhouette Books printing October 1990

BJ JAMES

married her high school sweetheart straight out of college, and soon found that books were delightful companions during her lonely nights as a doctor's wife. Her life is filled with her loving husband and family, pets, writing... and romance.

One

An eagle hovered in the slanting light of the setting sun, casting his random shadow over the sheer rock face of the mountain. Circling lower and lower over the valley floor, he searched the river's track. Suddenly, abandoning the languid guise of the hunt, he plunged through glittering rapids. Like a white-plumed thunderbolt he plundered the churning depths, snaring his prey in razor-sharp talons. With a cry, high and clear, he lifted his booty from the water's edge, streaking with it through the maze of towering trees and into the sun. From an aerie hidden in a distant crevasse rose the fierce, wild *scree!* of his mate, calling him home. With a riffle and curl of a wing he hitched a ride on the wind and soared over the mountain.

Christen traced the path of his flight until he was lost in the crimson haze of a cloud. She felt no pleasure in this rare sighting, no joy that this endangered creature had returned to her beloved North Carolina mountains. Instead her green eyes were dark and troubled. Her thoughts turned inward, as she sat huddled on a shelf of granite that jutted from the crest of Sunset Ridge.

She had come to the ridge in quiet desperation, to watch the setting sun, and lose herself in the distant tranquility of the valley. For the first time, her peaceful sanctuary failed her. She found in it neither comfort, nor solitude. A man who walked with her through her day, his face as somber as it was haunting, made mockery of her efforts.

There was no peace in the need he evoked, no discipline for the strange, lingering restlessness. Her trained, orderly mind skittered in forbidden directions and would not be quieted. She shivered, her body tensing in futile denial.

"Zachary!" His name was a low ragged cry. A swirling wind caught the hoarse sound, scattering it into the silence like falling leaves. It did not matter. There was no one to hear. Christen was alone.

Here in this special place, bathed in the fiery radiance of the setting sun, she struggled, not with flesh and blood, but with a memory. One deeply buried—until today, when the fleeting glimpse of a stranger with silver fire in his golden hair shattered all barriers. A tall man, slender but heavy shouldered, who moved with the long-limbed stride of a Viking . . . and played sudden havoc with her heart.

A stranger! Soon the streets would be filled with them, skiers passing through on their way to challenge the short, rough slopes of distant valleys. From the look of him he was a master skier. He was lean and fit, his step bold and confident. But were his eyes the ice-blue of a winter's sky? Would they burn with a glittering brilliance in triumph, or smolder bitterly in defeat? Was his face lean-cheeked and sun-darkened, the chiseled chin jutting stubbornly? She wondered if his smile would be rare and beautiful.

"This is madness!" Christen cried. A violent shake of her head dislodged the single tortoiseshell pin that anchored the heavy coil of her hair. Her mane of dark chestnut tumbled, unnoticed, like burnished silk about her shoulders. Her nails scored her palms, her fisted hands trembled. She had glimpsed a stranger. It was only in her foolish imaginings that he became something more.

A part of her knew it could not be Zachary Steele who walked the streets of Laurenceville. Zachary belonged in the past, in a life she had rejected. Five years had passed since she had made a choice, forfeiting a coveted residency at the prestigious Medical College of Brighton, and abandoning a promising career in internal medicine. Five years since the day she had fled from Zachary, leaving unanswered questions and bitterness behind.

Frightened and insecure, she had sought the simpler life of Laurenceville. It was incidental that she was the last surviving member of a Southern dynasty, returning to the village founded by her father's family. She was simply Christen Laurence, coming home to her *chosen* family—to the Sinclairs, Nathan and Greg, grandfather and grandson.

A small smile eased the grim set of her lips when she thought of Nathan. Her legal guardian since the death of her father, and the desertion of her mother for one of many lovers, left her penniless and alone at fifteen. He was much more than guardian, he was friend and mentor and self-appointed grandfather. He'd asked few questions when she'd abandoned her studies and her life in Brighton. Needing only the assurance that she was happy in her decision, he welcomed her back into his home and into his practice. Greg, the companion of her childhood, and no less wise than his grandfather, had asked nothing.

With their love and support, slowly she rebuilt her life. In time she managed to forget, and in time the dreams stopped.

The passion of the single night spent in Zachary's arms became a memory. The betrayal of a promise made long ago by a child to herself was forgiven.

She had emerged from her shell, embracing what life offered without reservation. There was triumph in her work, and there was tragedy. She had found a comfortable, easy love and lost it. And learned along the way the healing of grief. At last she faced her days with confidence, certain her yesterdays were forgotten.

Until a stranger stepped out of her memory.

"No!" In a gesture as desperate as it was angry, she flung her hair back from her face. For a moment she sat, head bowed, rigid as the granite beneath her. A calming breath rippled through her, trailing into a soft sigh. Long ago, at the tender age of fifteen, she had promised herself that love would never consume her. She would never be so blind, never so out of control, would never hunger for love as slavishly as her mother. She had vowed no man would ever become the center of her universe, commanding her heart and her passions. And no man had.

Not even Zachary.

Lifting her face to the wind, she let the chill of fall bathe her cheeks. Leaning her head back, she closed her eyes. Above her a gnarled pine swayed, its misshapen limbs rustling like a quiet sea. The rough-barked trunk at her back hummed in response. Locking away the tangled web of memories, willing herself to forget fatigue and secret loneliness, she listened to the wind. When only a sliver of sun was visible beyond the rim and shadows grew deeper, she knew it was time to go.

Rising slowly, she stood watching lights appear over the valley. Like a scattering of stars they dotted the creeping shadow of the mountain. Somewhere close by a mockingbird sang. His last sweet note hovered in the twilight, a reminder that tomorrow would always come.

Tomorrow, a new day. Christen smiled, her chin rose one proud, brave notch. She was not the confused, naive creature of the past, she hadn't been for a long time. She was a woman who had learned who she was and what she wanted. It was a security painfully achieved. No specter from the past was going to destroy it.

There would be other tall, fair-haired strangers. Perhaps there had been before and it was only in this time of overwork and worry that she had been vulnerable.

She wouldn't be again.

"Never."

Turning away from the valley she climbed to the dusty track above. By the time she was hurtling down the mountainside, the truck careening through the sharp zig and zag of switchbacks with a skill that would serve well in Monte Carlo, Christen's only concern was the evening ahead.

Two

Christen left her room, then moved quickly down a wide hall. The warm charm of the rambling old house bore little resemblance to the cold opulence of her ancestral home, the Laurence mansion, which had been shuttered and abandoned for more than a decade. For once Christen failed to appreciate the difference. She was dreadfully late after a long day at the clinic and a call over the mountain. And, she admitted ruefully, because of time squandered on Sunset Ridge.

Despite her hurry she paused at the head of the stairs, listening to the rush of music and conversations that rose from the library. Voices blended into an indistinct murmur, until Nathan laughed. The deep, hearty tone flowed from room to room, filling the house with its richness. Christen sighed in relief, delighted at the normal sound of it. A smile lit her face as she began to descend the stairs.

Her simple dress of jade silk clung and glided, then clung again like gleaming quicksilver, drawing subtle attention to the slender lines of her body. Its square, banded neckline offered a decorous but tantalizing glimpse of the creamy slope of her breasts. The dress was Nathan's favorite. She had chosen it for that reason, hoping its flattering lines would disguise the fatigue she hadn't quite shaken.

A hot bath had put a flush in her cheeks, a vigorous scrubbing took the dust of the mountain trail from her hair. Neither erased the weariness from her features. Nathan hadn't noticed that she'd gradually assumed more and more of the patient load, nor must he see the expense of it. She was younger, stronger, and in time she would adjust to the change. No one but herself need know of the throb at the base of her skull and the small of her back, a legacy of her jolting ride to call on a housebound patient.

As she crossed the foyer, a glance into a mirrored panel confirmed the sorcery of the dress. She looked refreshed, ready to join in another of Nathan's Friday gatherings.

At the library door she paused again. There were more guests than usual and no less varied. A wealthy lumberman dressed in a tuxedo was deep in discussion with a grizzled farmer whose mismatched suit was slick and shiny with age. On a sofa, a very tanned woman who divided her time between the ski slopes and the Riviera, listened raptly to an ancient lady whose skin was darkened from a half century of working the fields of her small valley farm. Christen knew a passion for needlepoint erased the barriers of age and life-style.

Chuckling, she scanned the crowd, wondering who but Nathan could bring together such disparate people so congenially. Seeking the wily host, her gaze touched one group after another. Her look slid negligently over a small cluster in a far, shadowed corner, dismissing them and turning away. Suddenly she stopped. With a sense of dread she turned back. For one heart-lurching moment, she thought she had gone mad.

He was there—the stranger with hair of silver and gold. His broad back, clad in an elegantly tailored dinner jacket, was turned to her as he bent over a handsome woman. *Zachary!*

Christen took a stumbling step back, one hand grasping at the doorjamb, the other shielding her eyes. Her head spun crazily. Her throat was dry. She gulped for air, unaware that the modest décolleté of her gown was threatened. Slowly, when she dared, she took her hand from her eyes. He was gone, swallowed up by the crowd. Perhaps he'd never been there at all.

"Dear heaven! What's wrong with me?" she whispered. It made no sense that after all these years she would suddenly begin to imagine Zachary at every turn. It was incredibly foolish. He would not be in Laurenceville. Certainly not in Nathan's home. Nathan had never known Zachary. He knew only that there had been a man, a once and nameless lover, who asked for more than she could give.

It could not be Zachary!

"It *must* not!" It was a moment before Christen was aware she spoke aloud. In that moment she was equally aware of curious glances. She'd stood conspicuously in the doorway too long. She should join the party before she conjured up a second golden Viking, or a dozen, and made a greater spectacle of herself.

"Ah ha!" A deep baritone boomed and she was caught in an embrace. "My lovely granddaughter has arrived. Now this lackluster party will come to life."

"Nathan," Christen murmured as she sagged against him. He seemed solid and strong. She could almost believe the little telltale signs of weakening were her imagination.

She wanted to believe but couldn't. Soon she must speak to him of his health, but not tonight. Instead she kissed him saying, "You sly fox. You never admit that I'm not really your granddaughter."

"That's because to me you are. Most old men are saddled with whatever they get. I got to choose. And I chose the best and the prettiest." He held her from him, studying her from arm's length. "The only problem is that right now you're so pale you look as if you've seen a ghost."

"For a moment today I thought I had," Christen muttered half aloud, half to herself.

"What?" A sudden blast of music forced Nathan to lean closer.

"Nothing, a poor joke."

"You really are white as chalk, my dear." Nathan stroked her cheek, his own face clouded with concern. "You saw Benjie today, didn't you? Seeing him always affects you. Dammit! I let you do too much."

"Nathan!" Her hand closed over his, holding it to her cheek before releasing it. "I saw Benjie. I hate what leukemia is doing to him, for no three-year-old child should suffer so. But it's part of my work, you can't protect me from it. I'll be fine. If I seem pale, it's because I skipped lunch."

"You haven't eaten in over twelve hours? Child! Child! When will you learn that even streamlined bodies like yours must have fuel?" He lifted his leonine head, his gaze probing the corners of the library. "I wanted you to meet someone, but later will do. The important thing is to get some food into you. Bell's setting up the buffet, I'm sure she'd fill a plate for you."

Christen looked toward the table where Nathan's housekeeper worked. "Perhaps breaking my fast would help."

"Feed that pretty body, then I promise we'll discuss the real cause of your pallor." Nathan turned away, then back. "I almost forgot, Hunter's here."

"Is he?" She asked, too distracted to react with her usual warmth to any news of Bell's son. Her mind still grappled with the implications of Nathan's promise. Only a stern reminder that he could know nothing of the stranger who haunted her memories calmed her.

Nathan peered down at her. "There's something wrong. When you're not interested in your big Cherokee friend..."

"Of course I'm interested in Hunter." Christen took a step back, disturbed by Nathan's keen inspection. He'd seen too much. "I'm just too famished to think of anything but food."

"Cross your heart?"

"Crossed." Christen silently asked forgiveness for the lie. "Now," she tapped the ruffled front of his shirt. "You attend to your guests, I'll attend to my stomach."

He stood watching her for what seemed an interminable time. Christen flashed her most radiant smile, waiting until he turned away to let the stiffening muscles of her face relax. Nathan was concerned, the very thing she hoped to avoid. What she wanted, more than anything, was that he be well and happy and as young and vigorous as he appeared to the untrained eye.

Fondly her gaze followed him, acknowledging that even now he was magnificent. Few would believe he had passed his seventy-seventh birthday. It was ironic that Nathan's dark hair had only rare strands of silver, and Zachary's, at thirty-four, had been as silver as it was gold. Impatiently she cut short the thought. This must stop! Every thought must not lead to Zachary and speculations were useless. A lot could change in five years. She had. Zachary would have.

He was an irrevocable part of her past, no more. He existed for her only in the images that possessed her mind. Hallucinations fueled by hunger and fatigue. These demons she could feed, then perhaps they would be quieted.

Obligatory greetings and conversations delayed her, but she finally arrived at Bell's side. As the American Indian woman fussed over her and filled a plate, Christen caught herself searching the crowd, desperately afraid she would find the golden-haired Viking, afraid she wouldn't.

Her eyes burned with her efforts, her throat ached. Her mouth seemed filled with cotton. When Bell pressed the heavily laden plate into her hand, she knew she could not eat. The room grew sultry. The throb at the base of her neck moved to her temples. A hot band encased her head like a twisted wire cutting into her skull. ''Bell,'' she muttered, her teeth clenched against the pain. ''I'll take this to the terrace.''

Pivoting hurriedly she nearly collided with two women of the village. Forcing a smile and planting a feathery kiss on each powdered cheek, she evaded their questions and managed to slip through an open door into the shadows of a small, deserted terrace. She sighed heavily as the crisp air cooled her skin. Setting the plate on a nearby table she stepped to the railing and looked out into the night.

A soft sound crackled somewhere in the darkness. A small animal scurried away in fright. A wisp of cigarette smoke curled over her head in a thread of mist, then vanished.

''That looked like an escape.'' The voice was deep, a little husky.

The cry Christen might have uttered froze on her tongue. There was a sudden sensation of falling through time, tumbling breathless and disoriented, not into the past, but into the foreseen. She knew then what her heart had always known, what her mind refused to accept. She had been waiting for this moment. Waiting for Zachary.

She turned slowly, peering into the gloom gathered on the far side of the terrace in lightless puddles. He was only a shape, darker, more solid than the blackness around him. "Zachary." She spoke in a whisper, but to her his name filled the terrace like a shout.

"Zachary." He laughed softly. "Only one other person in the world calls me that." A cigarette arched over the terrace wall, a shooting star of red. Then he was stepping into the light.

"Zachary," She said again like a broken record with the feeling of *déjà vu* that was all wrong. She and Zachary had never played a balcony scene. Urgent whispered conferences in darkened, antiseptic hospital corridors, yes, but never on a balcony. For one mad instant she thought she truly was hallucinating. But the delusion wouldn't work. When she shut her eyes and then opened them he was still there, watching her, a strange expression on his shadowed face.

Convincing herself he was real, her gaze wandered over him. He had changed a little. His heavy hair was still as gold as the sun, still streaked with shining silver. In a shaft of light falling through the open doors she saw that anger still sparkled like hot steel in the brilliant blue of his eyes. The anger! She felt the hot, fierce challenge of it. The same as it had been long ago.

"Still running away?" he drawled. The cruel thrust of his words was nearly lost in the soft inflection of his tone.

"Hardly," Christen retorted, her hackles rising as always when he baited her.

"Ahh." He chuckled but there was no humor in the sound. "Then I only imagined you almost bowled the ladies over in your hurry to get out of that room."

"I needed some air. Is there any harm in that?" She looked away from him but felt his compelling gaze on her. As the seconds ticked slowly away into silence she fought back a shiver as a small breeze drifted over her heated flesh. The beat of her heart was so heavy she wondered if he could hear it, or see its pulsing beneath the clinging silk of her dress.

"Since you don't run any more, what else has changed? Do you still fight for lost causes? Hurrah for the underdog and all sorts of good thoughts?" There was an unplundered bitterness beneath the silky amusement in his tone.

He did not speak of the party, nor her exit from the room. She wouldn't pretend he did. "I didn't run from you, Zachary."

"Didn't you?"

"I made a choice."

"*After* you climbed out of my bed." His voice dropped to a guttural jeer. "What happened, Christen? Were you afraid you couldn't be woman enough for me?" A gasp hissed through her teeth as the barb found its mark. "Ahh," he murmured. "From that little reaction, should I assume that after five years I've stumbled on the truth?"

There was a gentleness in him that was frightening. The quiet before the storm? The eye of the hurricane? Christen lashed out into the threatened calm. "Don't assume!"

"What else was there for me but assumption, Christen? I awoke and discovered a note. Stark phrases that made little sense. Words from a frightened child, not the vibrant woman I had loved. Can you even begin to imagine how it was to know that I was your first, to see you come alive beneath my touch as you never had before, then have you leave me?"

"Stop it! You're giving a casual encounter more importance than it merits."

"Is that all it was for you?" Zachary asked almost too softly to be heard, but the thread of violence was still there.

"Yes!" She spun away, turning from him, afraid that even in the darkness he would read the truth on her face. "That's all."

"Then why did you run, Christen? If it meant so little?"

"For the last time, I didn't run."

"Who are you lying to, little coward? To yourself, or to me?"

"Neither. I simply realized I'd made some wrong choices." With her hand she clasped the nape of her neck, glad of the reality of an ache that kept her from sliding into the hurt and confusion of the past. "I'd made mistakes that needed correcting."

"And making love with me was one of them?" There was something strange in him. Something she couldn't fathom.

"It was...." Christen shut her mouth with an audible click. She need not defend herself, not now, not to Zachary. After five years he stepped out of the shadows and back in her life and she was on trial again. Once he'd almost overwhelmed her with his powerful passions, but this time she knew her own worth, her own strengths.

"You didn't answer my question." He was moving closer. So close she could see the tiny lines that etched his eyes. So close he seemed to tower over her.

"What questions?" For all her mental protestations, she felt her control slipping with each step he took. Zachary was a dangerous man. Once he had threatened the creed that had been the basis for the rebirth of a young, shattered life. In all the years since her mother's desertion, only he had stormed the walls of the sanctuary she vowed to hold inviolate. In his arms she had learned the meaning of rapture, and discovered promises were like thistles scattered in a whirlwind of passion. As she looked at him now, remembering with a sinking heart all she wanted to forget, she knew he would always mean danger to her.

"I asked you, Christen, if you still fought impossible causes?"

It was the same old argument. The years of separation might not have ever been. "Coming back to practice with Nathan was not an impossible cause."

"It was for one so gifted. Perhaps you felt hemmed in by the city, but you loved the hospital and the training. You thrived on it. For a little while it was your life and no lie can change it." He spoke in a low compelling rasp, and the cold glitter in his piercing eyes dared her to deny his truths.

Beneath the force of his gaze her last barriers against the past collapsed. A tidal wave of memories assaulted her, and Christen found herself reliving their early days as residents, the grueling hours, the weariness, the pain of failure, the giddiness of success. Each day filled with fear. Each day a challenge. How many times had she sat, sharing a cup of coffee with Zachary, respected colleague and treasured friend, too drained to do more than smile fatuously, yet never so utterly alive.

Her eyes drifted shut, a frown tugged at her brow. Zachary was indeed a dangerous man. In a matter of minutes he had gone for the jugular and laid bare her secrets and her regrets. "Enough!" There was no rancor in her, only resignation and a deep wariness. "It's an old, old argument, Zachary. One settled and done. We were friends and for a night we were lovers, but our concept of medicine and the plan for our lives were never the same. Your choice was a specialty, a city practice. I chose general medicine and Laurenceville." Her unwavering gaze met his. "I never regretted the choice, I never will. So leave it."

"As you wish," he said, abandoning the subject with a willingness that was suspect. He moved closer, his nearness and the subtle scent of his cologne unsettling her more. His hand closed over hers, his thumb moving over her fingers. "Five years and still no ring? I recall when you left the hospital, left me, for this wonderland, there was a vague mention of a boy."

"A man!" Christen interjected, pulling her hand from his.

"A man," Zachary nodded unperturbed. "Your first love. Yet, you never married him."

Christen looked beyond the terrace, blinking back unexpected tears. She had been dishonest in using Greg as her buffer against Zachary. But in time the lie became truth. Greg, her first love, the love of her childhood, became her last love. Her lost love.

Through her unfocused gaze she saw that the party had spilled out into the garden. Nathan was there, looking deceptively young and fit in the flattering light of a lantern. Christen's heart contracted as she watched him walk, tall and gracefully, among his flowers. Greg would have looked very much like him one day.

"There was a logging accident?" The bitterness was gone from Zachary. She heard a surprising compassion.

"Yes." Her answer was toneless, devoid of the sense of failure she felt.

"Nathan told me about his grandson, the loaded truck, the faulty chain," Zachary said softly.

Christen drew a sharp, startled breath. Greg's face rose in her mind. Not as she wanted to remember it, but as she had last seen him. No longer handsome and laughing, but battered beyond recognition and her help. "He was standing by the truck when the chain snapped." Christen looked away. She could not look into Zachary's handsome face remembering the travesty Greg's had become. "We grew up together. There were three of us, the Musketeers, Greg and I, and Hunter Slade. Greg was our champion. He was bigger and older and many years wiser. No one dared call Hunter a half-breed in his presence and no matter what I needed, Greg was always there. When he needed me, there was nothing I could do. Nathan's wife and only son had died with Greg's mother in a car crash. Greg was all the family Nathan had left, and I couldn't do this one single thing for either of them. I couldn't keep Greg.''

''You always took it hard when you couldn't 'keep' a patient.''

''Greg was more than a patient. I loved him,'' she said brokenly and braced for a cruel remark, an ugly comparison of choices and men and boys. The words never came. Nearby a tree frog began to sing, a prophesy of rain. She listened to the soothing sound, then bowed her head, speaking in a low voice. ''One day he was healthy and happy, the next . . .'' She couldn't go on. There was nothing more to say, not to Zachary. Clasping her hands behind her back she lifted her face again to the stars.

Zachary pulled another cigarette from his jacket pocket, reconsidered, and then tossed it away. There was an edge of regret in the deep breath he drew but he said nothing. The subject was closed.

In the library the music changed. Christen recognized Nathan's favorite song. She searched the garden expecting to see him hurrying inside to dance a bar or two. Instead, Nathan, who was never still when he could dance, sat alone in the shadows of the gazebo. A feeling of dread coiled up her spine and settled like ice in her chest, for in the shifting light he was a fragile old man.

Suspicion nibbled at the back of her mind. An unformed thought, the missing piece that would complete the puzzle, the connection between the kind, old man who had helped her put her life back together, and the brash young one had nearly destroyed it. "Zachary." She faced him. The expensive scent of his cologne, as elegant as it was masculine, drifted about her but she was hardly aware of it now. "What brought you here?"

"I should think that's obvious."

"Is it?"

"I thought so," he parried. "I'm Nathan's guest."

"How do you know him?"

"We met a few months ago."

"He never mentioned it."

"Should he?" With a quick flare of anger his stare caught her, holding her, waiting. "Would my name mean anything to him?"

"No." The word was a soundless quirk of her lips. An imperceptible tilting of her head sent her hair sliding in ripples over her shoulders. Zachary's name would mean nothing to Nathan. In all the time she'd fought herself and her memories, she hadn't once spoken his name.

Nathan was a gregarious man. His friendships were instant, varied, and often surprising. A new face in their home was never unexpected. It was natural that once he met Nathan, Zachary would be here. That was the purpose of the Friday gatherings. Nathan liked his friends, he liked having them near. He would draw a man of Zachary's caliber into his coterie of friends, never understanding what it did to her. "No," she said aloud. "There's absolutely no reason Nathan should mention you."

"I thought not."

There was a strange undercurrent in him. Christen had the inexplicable impression his comment had a double edge. She spoke of the past, Zachary of both past and present. What had he left unsaid? She looked at him, trying to pierce the veil of shadows that cloaked him. "But this is not some wild coincidence and you're not *just* one of Nathan's guests, are you?"

Zachary shrugged. "Nathan invited me. I came."

"All the way from the bright lights and your city life to attend a party in the 'boondocks' as you once called it?"

"Yes."

"I don't believe you."

"Not believing me seems to be a habit with you." The anger that simmered constantly beneath the surface flicked again in his voice. He stepped away, his gaze sweeping coldly over her. "This conversation has come full circle." A crooked smile that left his eyes untouched tilted a corner of his mouth. "Some things change, some don't. There's little need in wasting our breath discussing them. Now, if you'll excuse me, I promised a dance to a charming Ms. Felicity Davenport." He bowed slightly, with an old world dignity, and turned away.

Christen watched him go. He was right, there were things that never changed. Zachary for one. He was still hard and lean, and taller than most men at six foot three. Born in the waterfront slums of Brighton, he still moved with the watchful care of the street fighter he'd been. It would always be a part of him. Not even the gilding of his bootstrap success could obliterate the odd mingling of courtliness and the cocky, streetsmart toughness she found fascinating. No matter what was in his heart, he looked the same. And he was still the best in his field of medicine. Her startled gasp was barely contained by cold fingers clamped over her lips. *The best in his field!*

"Zachary!" She called after him.

He half turned, one hand in his pocket, pulling his jacket aside. The white shirt with its multitude of tiny tucks only served to accentuate his masculinity. Softly he asked, "You wanted something, Christen?"

"Why are you really here?"

"You finally asked. Blunt and straight. No frills, no hedging. I wondered how long it would take." The anger that brought old habits of the waterfront to the surface was gone. There was something new in his face, something she couldn't read.

"It's a logical question," she said, ignoring the subtle barb.

"Very logical."

"A logical question deserves a logical answer. Of all the places, in all the world, why are you here, in Nathan's house." She swallowed, hating the husky sound of her voice she added, "Our home."

Zachary's gaze lingered interminably on her mouth. He started to speak, then paused. She saw heavy shoulders shrug beneath his close-fitting jacket. Light tangled in his hair as he shook his head. "I think I should leave this to Nathan."

"Tell me, Zachary."

"You'll know when Nathan's ready. No sooner. You finally asked your question. Now I have one of my own. For two years, before he died, you lived here in this house with Greg Sinclair. Yet you never married. Why Christen?" He held her riveted by his fierce intensity. A leaden silence, not meant to be filled, fell between them. His question wanted no answer. Not yet, not here on a small, dark terrace with dozens of revelers beyond the light.

"No. Not now. Not here," he said. "But I'll have my answer before I leave Laurenceville." He bowed again, the slightest bend of his waist, and beneath his hardness Christen saw the nuance of inherent gentility. "You must excuse me. I did promise Ms. Davenport a dance."

Long after he disappeared into the library Christen stared after him. She had been a quivering mass, her nerves strained, her mind set on denial. Now she was simply numb, her thoughts focused against her will on Zachary.

She wandered absently to the railing, her arms crossed over her breasts, her hands clutching her arms against the cold she did not feel. Instinctively she turned her gaze to the garden, seeking Nathan. The gazebo and the grounds were deserted. The party would be breaking up soon. He was inside with his guests.

Christen thought ruefully of the food Bell had served her. An attractive array of her favorites, but the little appetite she might have managed had flown away. She considered a glass of wine, but rejected the thought as folly. She drank little and dared not cloud her judgment. This night of all nights she needed her wits about her.

Sinking down onto a chaise lounge she slid off her shoes and drew her legs beneath her. Her hair spread over the cushion as she leaned her head against it. With eyes closed, she let her mind range, probing the past, addressing the present, pondering the future. Her brows were drawn down, her full lower lip was caught between her teeth as she plundered her mind, seeking her own answers to questions that echoed in her thoughts. Why had Zachary come here? How had his unlikely friendship with Nathan come to be? What was its significance?

Christen's hand brushed over her forehead. The brief touch, cool and surprisingly steady, served as a palliative, restoring a semblance of equilibrium. She turned her attention to the night sky and the stars scattered over it. They always seemed so close. As a child, she had tried to reach out and touch one, wanting to draw it down, to cradle it in her palm like a diamond. Even in those very young years she found solace in the night. Now, as then, the darkness soothed her. Like a cloak of velvet it embraced her, smoothed the jagged edges of the world and offered consolation for her troubles. She drifted, letting her mind slowly slip free of its fetters. Softly she sighed, and there was only the night.

She had no idea how much time had passed when the familiar sound of a tinkling bell roused her. "Bell?"

"Who else walks to music of silver?" The housekeeper spoke of the silver bell clasped to a thin chain about her ankle. A bell so tiny and delicate its sound could be heard only at close range. Christen couldn't remember a day in all the years she'd known Bell that the soft musical tinkling had not accompanied her step. Bell touched Christen's shoulder. "You should come in now. He's asked for you twice."

"Nathan?"

"Of course. Who else?"

"I thought maybe . . . maybe Hunter." The quaver in her voice was unnatural, an alien thing for the self-assured woman she thought herself.

"My son asked once, but he saw how tired you appeared and chose to wait until later to speak with you." Bell Slade spoke with the curious formality of one whose first language differed from the language she spoke.

Christen knew it was the language of Bell's people, the Cherokee. Swinging her feet to the floor she smiled her thanks for the scattered shoes Bell retrieved. "His exhibit was a success?"

"The reviews were good. There were commissions. One special one, a bronze, he wants to discuss with you. But not until he's been home awhile and cleared the city sludge from his brain."

Christen chuckled. Hunter, part English by birth, pure Cherokee in his heart, could have surrounded himself with wealth, but elected to live in simple isolation on a mountaintop.

"I know," Bell chuckled, too. "My son's face is his father's, his English name means 'dweller in the valley,' but his heart belongs to the mountains and to the Cherokee."

"And his talents." Christen thought of those huge, rough hands that could coax magic from the clay he molded or the stone he carved.

"Christen, you procrastinate." The Indian woman touched her shoulder again, gently, but insistently. Her innate calm did not waver as she asked, "Why are you so reluctant to rejoin the party that you dwell on such trivial discussions?"

"Hunter's talent is trivial?"

"Of course not." Bell refused to rise to the bait of Christen's teasing. "But it's not Hunter who keeps you hiding on a darkened terrace like a child. The new guest from the city is a handsome man. He has the look of strength, but he's not an ogre to frighten a woman like you. It's been a long time since you were a young woman-child frightened of men, Christen." Before Christen could make the shocked protestations that they both knew would ring false, the housekeeper admonished softly, "The doctor sees that you're tired. He worries too much already. So smile. Come face what you must. The evening will end soon."

Bell never argued. She simply stated the obvious—and often the less obvious—and retreated as she did now, with only the bell to mark her silent footsteps. There were times when Christen suspected the woman was guided by a mystical native wisdom, born of her heritage.

Beyond the empty terrace, deep in the woods an owl called, mocking her fancy. Christen smiled again. Stretching her arms high over her head, she flexed cramped muscles, easing the tension from them. As she stood, the smile faded. Nathan waited for her there beyond the open doors, and so did Zachary.

She still felt the weight of his unreadable gaze on her and heard the undercurrent beneath his words. He was Nathan's friend, Nathan's guest, but something unfinished had begun again tonight. In the end, whether it was love or hate that drew them together, she knew it would be only the two of them. Only Zachary and herself.

Christen shivered, not from the temperature that had cooled as the night deepened, but in premonition. Scattered clouds gathered by a high-flown wind scudded over the moon and blanketed the stars. The lightless sky seemed to hold secret some dark future. But the future need not be dark. There had been troubled times before. She had endured. She would again.

As she crossed the terrace, her step was sure. For the first time in this day of mental chaos, her cheerful good nature returned. She would let nothing spoil this night for Nathan, but soon she would go to him and face with him the problem of his faltering health.

Pausing in the light that fell beyond the open door, feeling strangely warmed by it, she knew that she could deal with Zachary. She did not try to fool herself that it would be easy. Zachary was a vital man, he was excitement and sensual magnetism, and once he had threatened everything she believed in.

It didn't matter why he was here. It didn't matter what happened between them. She was older now, and wiser, and she would survive. "No matter what," she whispered softly, letting the music engulf her as she entered the library where Nathan and Zachary waited.

Three

―――

"Christen! I wondered where you'd gotten to." Nathan appeared out of a crowd, a look of pleasure on his face. He caught her hands in both of his. "Better? You ate well?"

"As much as I could." She salved her conscience by convincing herself the evasion was not really a lie. "You worry about me too much."

"And you work too hard," Nathan countered. "But that should be remedied soon." He was watching the guests as he spoke. Christen knew whom it was he sought among them. With a sinking feeling she watched his face light with discovery. His smile widened. There was a boyish delight about him. "There he is by the bar. Come. I want you two to meet, or I should say meet again. He was a fellow resident of yours at Brighton. Imagine the coincidence. Small world!" He laughed and tugged her hand, beginning to weave his way through the room. She could only nod and smile as she passed people by. Nathan seemed to have a surge of energy.

The frail man she'd seen in the garden was not the man who unwittingly led her back to Zachary.

"He's one of the finest young doctors I've met in a long while." This was tossed over his shoulder in more than his usual enthusiasm for a new friend. He was gleefully pleased with himself and with Zachary.

"Nathan." Christen tried to slow him. She felt like the caboose on a speeding train. Despite the reassertion of her confidence in the darkness of the terrace, she needed a moment to prepare for a public confrontation.

"You had to see his promise in training. The two of you must have been tops in your group."

"Where did you meet this paragon?"

"Brighton, of course."

Of course. Brighton, Zachary's home, Christen thought as she was rushed headlong toward him. "Nathan, would you tell me, please, when you were at Brighton?"

"That will take a little explaining."

"I'm beginning to think it will."

"It's a terrible shame, a sharp mind going to waste." His excitement over Zachary was underscored again by his tone. "Not to worry. This mountain air and a few long days at the clinic should blow the cobwebs from his mind. Why he didn't know he wasn't cut out for the silliness of a society practice is beyond me."

"Nathan!" With a sense of panic giving her strength, Christen pulled him to a halt. Her heart was pounding so hard she feared it would leap from her throat. "What on earth are you muttering about?"

"Was I muttering?" His heavy brows lifted in surprise. "I was, wasn't I?" He chuckled, a look of wicked delight on his face. "Shows how much we need him, doesn't it?" he declared, and drew her helplessly through the crowd. Before she was ready, their journey ended and she was face to face with Zachary.

"Zack," Nathan drew her forward, presenting her like a proud parent. "My granddaughter, Christen."

Zachary set the glass he held on a nearby table and took Christen's cold, left hand in both of his. He did not smile. Instead his glittering gaze slid over her, touching on the extreme pallor of her cheeks, lingering just a fraction too long at the full slope of her breasts before moving down the length of her too slender body, seeking every change the terrace shadows had obscured. Leisurely, with an unhurried deliberation, that pale, piercing stare returned to her face to capture her emerald gaze. A small smile touched his lips, leaving the hard planes of his face unaltered. "It's been a long time, Christen."

"Yes." She dared only the single word. His grip on her hand was sweetly painful, the thumb that stroked her bare ring finger scorched her flesh as his caresses had once scorched her body. Her breasts tightened under the return of his plundering stare and desire jolted through her. Mindlessly her gaze dropped to his mouth as she wondered what it would be like to kiss him again, to lose herself in the intoxicating male scent and taste of him, and end the loneliness of her nights in his arms.

The soft stroke of his thumb slowed, stopped, waited. Christen drew her dazed contemplation from that handsome, sardonic mouth. What she saw as her gaze locked inexorably with his sent a tremor down her spine. He knew what his touch had done to her. A frigid satisfaction was not quite hidden by the hostile glitter of his eyes. Her hand jerked convulsively but his crushing response held her fast.

At her barely suppressed gasp he murmured, "Sorry." Lifting her hand to his mouth he brushed her palm with his lips, his tongue warm and moist against her flesh. "I had forgotten how delicate you really were beneath the layers of hospital whites.''

She felt her face flush with heat. Once as he had drawn her to him, his marauding hands exploring every inch of her bare flesh, he had whispered almost reverently of delicacy beneath the camouflage of hospital dress. Swift anger swept through her. Zachary was doing everything in his power to unnerve her. Warning signals of imminent danger turned the cold that coiled in her spine to tensile steel. She would not be drawn into his game. ''My dress is hardly hospital white,'' she said with all the regal aloofness she could summon.

A tactical error, she realized too late, as that sapphire gaze plundered again the silk-covered secrets of her body. ''How well I know,'' Zachary chuckled wickedly.

Remembering that he still held her hand in his, she tugged it free, tucking it firmly behind her. The touch of his lips, the caress of his tongue still pulsed there like an electric current.

Beyond them the music ended. Christen was stunned that what seemed an eternity had been only a small passage of time. None of the surrounding conversations had stopped, no dancers paused in mid-step to stare. Nathan, usually so astute, beamed with ungovernable pride at what he must think was the reunion of friends.

Breathing a sigh of relief Christen stepped back from Zachary. Slipping her hand through Nathan's arm, she asked quietly, ''What brings you to visit Laurenceville, Zachary?''

''It's more than a visit, Christen.'' Nathan patted her hand where it rested in the crook of his arm. ''Zack's agreed to spend the winter here in Laurenceville, working in the clinic with you.''

"Working? With me?" She dropped Nathan's arm and turned to stare blankly at him.

"Honey," Nathan linked his arms at her waist, drawing her into his embrace, but even his bulk could not stem the dread that crept over her. "I've not been well. You've known it for some time. I've watched you work yourself into the ground, covering for me, not admitting to yourself or to anyone that it was true. So, I've had to admit it for both of us. I haven't pulled my weight in a long time, but I was better than no help at all. I saw no hope for us. Then I met Zack."

"Where exactly did you meet?" She looked at Zachary and found him watching her. She had felt the color drain from her face and knew she must look ghastly against the once-flattering jade of her dress.

"We met at the Medical Center. Carey Brown called in Zack for a second opinion," Nathan said.

"The Medical Center? A second opinion?" She sounded like a parrot.

"Christen, my last fishing trip with Carey wasn't a fishing trip at all. I admitted myself into the Medical Center so he could check me out. I had to find out why I was having one cold after another. Why each lingered longer than the one before it, leaving me with a cough that threatened to tear my lungs out."

"No. Oh please, no!" Christen whispered. She was suddenly, painfully alert. Nathan's every word was stamped on her mind like a brand. Somewhere in the wasteland of her thoughts she heard the music begin. The room filled with dancing couples. She looked wildly about her wondering how they could dance and laugh.

"Honey, listen, hear what I'm saying." Nathan stroked her hair, soothing her as he had when she was a hurting teenager. "It's not as bad as it could be. I simply need to get away. These old lungs need a rest, some time in sunshine. Just a few months, then I'll be fine. I need this rest, Zack needs a change, you need a partner. It was too perfect to miss."

"Nathan." She cupped her palm about his cheek, looking into his face, seeing the ravages of illness she hadn't wanted to see. "Why didn't you tell me? I could have done something."

He kissed her palm, the same that Zachary had kissed, and took her hand in his. "I didn't have to tell you, honey. You knew. We both did in our hearts. There's not a damn thing more you could do than you have. Carey's tests and Zack's consult were simply a confirmation. We all knew another winter here would take its toll, but I also knew I couldn't leave you here alone. The clinic is too much for one person."

"My sabbatical and Nathan's need coincided. Wouldn't you agree that it was providence, Christen?" There was an unmistakable challenge in Zachary's voice, daring her to protest when they both knew she couldn't. Not when it was Nathan's life that lay in the balance.

"I should've given you some warning, Christy-girl. But I know you. You would've insisted you could manage alone. When I discovered Zack was an old friend, when he said you'd done well together in training..." Nathan grasped Zachary's hand, drawing it to Christen's. "Well, as he said, it was providence."

Zachary's fingers closed hard over hers, the short nails biting into her flesh. The message in his icy blue eyes squelched her denial. She knew by the grim look in them that Nathan made light of his symptoms. Another winter here might be a death sentence.

"Zack can have the rooms across from yours. They've been gathering dust for too many years. Bell will enjoy cooking for a hearty appetite again."

"Perhaps Zachary would prefer his own place," Christen said, slipping her hand from Zachary's grasp. "There must be friends he would want to entertain."

"Lovers?" Zachary suggested, the familiar, sardonic smile that touched only his lips firmly entrenched.

"I was going to suggest that your wife might like to join you." His ring finger was bare, but she knew it could mean nothing.

"I have no wife, Christen. I've made no commitments. Not yet. I can't until certain things are settled."

"Our deal is settled, isn't it?" Nathan asked with relish. "You two will live and work together while I follow doctors' orders and lounge in the sun for a few months."

"Christen?" The warning was still in Zachary's tone.

"Yes," she whispered, hemmed in, caught like a bird in a barbed trap. Struggle only drove the barb deeper. "It's settled."

"Terrific." The color in Nathan's cheeks was high, his eyes were bright, but Christen knew this aura of good health wouldn't last. Not through the winter, when the coughing came. "Now," he gestured expansively. "We introduce Zack to our guests, and tell them our plans."

"Nathan!" Christen clutched at his arm. "Can't that wait? At least until things are arranged?"

"What's to arrange? And what better time than now?" The older man frowned down at her. "Second thoughts, honey?"

"Of course not," she said too quickly.

"Good, girl." Nathan beamed. "Have you ever seen anyone like her Zack?"

"Never," Zachary said and embers of a long-dimmed fire smoldered in his look.

Nathan clapped Zachary on the back, saying, "You two wait right here. I'll tell Bell, then we'll make the announcement."

When Nathan left them, Christen could find nothing to say, nor could she bring herself to look into those accusing eyes. The dark moment was broken by Zachary's exaggerated applause.

"Well, done, Christen," he said as his hands fell to his sides. "No one would ever know how much you hate this. You're quite an actress." There was a diamond hardness in him as he leaned slightly closer, his mouth almost brushing her temple as he murmured, "But then, you always were, weren't you?"

He left her then, standing alone in the crowd. She wrapped her arms about her waist, holding back the spasm that twisted her slender frame, bracing herself for the worst.

The rest of the evening passed in a blur. Christen walked and moved like a zombie, listening to the announcement, answering endless questions. She saw Bell's puzzled frown and felt Hunter's speculative gaze following her. With her mind in a jumbled turmoil, she avoided them both, not ready to deal either with the questions they would ask, or with the help they would willingly give. Hunter possessed the same intuitive understanding of her moods as Bell. She sensed both mother and son were concerned by her unusual quietness, but neither approached her. Nor would they. When the time came—and it would—when she needed friends, Christen knew they would be there.

Hunter had taken his leave—kissing her cheek, promising to call to discuss his latest commission—and Bell was clearing away the table, when Christen seized her own chance to escape. Only one guest remained, a local salesman, who held Nathan and Zachary in his clutches with a tale of his latest success.

Forgetting any shred of dignity, Christen fled up the stairs and down the hall, slamming the door of her room behind her. Leaning against it, her breasts heaving from her exertion, she was surprised that the hand that clutched the knob was steady. There was no visible evidence of the torment of her memories.

Memories of Zachary... the boy from the slums of the waterfront, the street fighter, the marine. Tough. Quick. Restless. Intelligent. Dangerous. Dedicated student, compassionate physician, brilliant diagnostician. Her best friend in the world beyond Laurenceville. Her first and only lover. Her lost friend. Her enemy.

A shudder seized her as she remembered the cruel, bitter smile, the cold hostility. "But he never hurt me," she muttered hoarsely. "The hurt that was done I did, to myself and to him."

Wearily she pushed away from the door, stripping the dress from her shoulders as she crossed the room. Clad only in a camisole and tap pants she sat at her dressing table, running a brush idly through her hair. "If it's revenge he wants at this late date, I can handle it." Tossing her brush aside she stood, leaning on her hands, staring into her own reflected eyes. "Perhaps I deserve it."

But what if he wants something else? Christen? What will you do then? Her own eyes questioned her, waiting for an answer she didn't have.

With a sudden spurt of wild energy she strode to her closet, chose a pair of jeans and a heavy shirt. She pulled her hair into a ponytail. Within minutes she was in her truck, a baseball cap perched on her head, her sneaker-clad foot pressed hard against the throbbing accelerator. She would drive like the wind, taking the curves of the deserted road with reckless abandon. Maybe then she could escape the question in the reflection of her own eyes.

"Ohh!" Christen moaned as she tiptoed up the stairs. She was tired, but reveled in the mind-dulling aches. Her punishing drive had accomplished its purpose. Her shoulders and wrists were numb from wrestling the heavy truck through precarious turns, her legs were leaden from the constant pull of braking and acceleration. She had found the antidote for errant thoughts.

She was thankful for the single-minded concentration needed now to lift one foot and put it quietly in front of the other. Bell slept at the far end of the house, and Nathan beyond the stairs in a ground floor suite. As she climbed the stairs she was careful to make no sound that might wake them. She was at her door when, behind her, Zachary opened his.

"Do you have any idea what time it is?" He demanded in a low, insistent voice.

"I beg your pardon?" She swung about to face him, unprepared for the sight that greeted her. He was dressed for bed in only the trousers of his pajamas. A robe, obviously thrown on in haste, hung open, exposing the breadth of his bare chest. A thin, gold chain glinted at his neck. An angel, once the mark of his street gang and later of survival and success, was almost hidden by a heavy, curling pelt that dusted his naked skin with its own gossamer of gold.

"It's two o'clock. Where in hell have you been?"

"It's none of your business. Lower your voice. You'll wake the house with your shouting."

"Do you think anyone can sleep when you're racing over the mountain like a mad woman?"

"Nobody worries about me, Zachary."

"Don't they? Or are you too insensitive to realize it?"

"Please!" Pushing back her cap she massaged her aching temple with a forefinger. Her day had been too long and too disrupted to deal with a high-handed male. "I would appreciate it if you'd keep your voice down."

"Then come inside where we can speak freely."

"No."

"Suit yourself, but you're going to hear what I think of tonight's little performance, either in my room, or here in the hall."

"Don't kid yourself," Christen snapped. "I couldn't care less what you think."

"My room or the hall. The choice is yours." He folded his arms over his chest. She had seen the obdurate gesture many times.

"This is blackmail!"

"Blackmail?"

"Dammit! You know I don't want to disturb Nathan. If he had any inkling of trouble between us, wild horses wouldn't drag him away. Because of your stubbornness he'd spend the winter coughing his lungs out."

"My stubbornness?" He clucked his tongue and lifted a brow in mock astonishment. For a fleeting instant Christen thought she saw the ghost of a smile.

"All right!" She snatched the cap from her head, flinging it to the floor in frustration. "You win. But when Nathan's gone the rules of this game will change."

"Temper. If you're not careful someone might think my presence upsets you."

She shot him a malignant look of pure disgust and strode angrily past him. When the door closed behind her she whirled on him. "What the hell gave you the idea that you upset me?"

"What indeed?" He laughed softly. "You've been as jumpy as a rabbit all evening, and I distinctly remember you used to have a little color here and here." He stroked each cheek with his thumb.

Christen drew back from his touch, then cringed at his chuckle. With a jerk, she moved toward the window, putting a wall of distance between them. "You overrate yourself," she flung back at him. "I've been fine all evening."

"Really? Perhaps you should ask the big Indian who watched you like a hawk. I thought he was going to sweep you up and away out of whatever danger that threatened."

"Hunter?"

"Once I feared for my scalp. An unusual fierceness in a man who creates such beauty."

"You know Hunter's work?" Her astonishment put her off stride.

"I know it." He nodded.

That took the wind completely out of the sails of her anger. Without it to spur her, she could find nothing more to say.

"Close your mouth, Christen. Have the good grace to hide your surprise."

Christen felt the flags of embarrassment rise in the cool pallor of her cheeks. She must have been gawking at him like some silly fool. "I never realized you had an interest in art."

"There was a great deal you didn't want to realize."

"You have to admit discovering you're an admirer of art is a bit astonishing."

"A street kid is too crude to appreciate talent?"

"No, of course not," she said a little too quickly.

"Ahh, Christen, Christen," he shook his head mockingly. "Have you sat complacently here in your safe, isolated haven and become a prim little snob?"

He was moving closer, his gaze riveted on her, each gliding step as silent as a panther's. Christen took an involuntary step back. She had the disturbing thought that her mental image of his step was apt. He was stalking her. She wanted to take a second step back, but instincts, honed to a primal intensity, warned that a show of intimidation would be her undoing. If he had proof of the power of his attraction, nothing would stop him, and she would be lost. She had walked away from him once. Could she again?

"Have you become a snob, my beautiful Christen?" he asked huskily, a small frown flickering over his features.

Refusing to acknowledge his accusation, she forced herself to stand, waiting, watching each graceful, measured tread. She would not let herself be caught up in this cat-and-mouse game he was playing with her. He was still wickedly attractive, and an element of intriguing mystery added to it. Falling under his spell would be like dancing barefoot through flames, and she had no desire to be burned. This was a stranger, not the Zachary of her past. She drew a wavering breath and stiffened her spine. A slight tilt of her head brought her gaze to his. Green fire collided with blue, locking and holding as he stopped before her.

With the tip of one finger he touched the throbbing pulse in the hollow of her throat. Stroking the soft flesh, he traced the curve of her neck to the rounded jut of her chin. "One of the most unexpected things about you was your sense of fairness, your generosity in judging people. Not many young girls of your background would have given a poor street kid the time of day. But that was once upon a time, and things change." He held her chin firmly, but there was no need. She would not have turned away. He bent nearer, his breath warm against her cheek, the tip of the exploring finger caressed and tugged at the fullness of her lower lip. "They did change, didn't they?"

"Stop it!" She wrenched away, the swirling mass of her ponytail tangling in his upraised hand. Frantically she pulled it free.

"I wondered how long it would take, " he said lazily. "You really hate for me to touch you, don't you?" To prove his point, his hand curled about her neck, catching again in her hair.

Christen swayed, her body keening for his touch even as she fought to deny it. "No!" She whispered to herself more than to Zachary. Her eyes clouded, her hands knotted into fists. "Please."

Zachary laughed, an explosive, humorless sound wrenched unexpectedly from the dark, hidden depths of a ruthless conscience. "Please, Christen?" Her name was a guttural growl, so low she barely heard it. His hand at her nape was steel drawn into a velvet glove, coaxing her to him, slowly, gently. "Is this the little daredevil who spends half the night driving like a mad woman trying to outrun her desires?"

She meant to hold herself aloof from the intimate touch of his body as he drew her closely against him. She fought the wildfire that was spreading through her by thinking of the ruthless thrust of his questions, the latent cruelty that simmered in him. She meant to hide her struggle from him, but her stony expression faltered, betraying her.

The hard blue glitter of his stare widened, startled by the subtle change in her. The withering disdain softened visibly before he could mask it beneath narrowed lids. The strained set of his shoulders tightened like a man punched in the gut. A barely suppressed groan slipped through the grim slash of his mouth. The muscles in his thighs rippling against her left little doubt that his response was far more than simple anger.

Her shocked gasp sent her unbound breast rising to brush against him, the heat of him searing her body as if it were naked against his flesh. Her lashes drifted down to rest lightly on her cheeks, shielding her eyes. He muttered a low rasping curse, his hand winding in her hair, lifting her face to his.

"Look at me," he half commanded, half pleaded. "Dammit! I said look at me."

Languidly, with no will of her own, she obeyed, lifting her gaze, heavy with the need of five lonely years, to his.

"Christen? My God!" He murmured in an uncertain tone. "Christen?...Darling?"

Darling? Christen stiffened. His endearment awakened her from a dream as harshly as a dash of cold water. Dear heaven! What was she doing? Suddenly she hurtled back, trying to free herself, but he refused to release her.

His hand at her neck became an unwelcome weight. Her temper flared, fueled by a staggering fear. Her face was ashen. She had been flushed by heat and was now icy cold. Fear died as quickly as it came, but not the anger. It burned in her with a consuming flame, but her voice was like an arctic wind. "Don't be a fool, Zachary."

The cutting revulsion in her carefully enunciated demand found its mark. Zachary stopped. His grip tightened, suggesting he would like nothing better in this moment than to break her neck. She refused to sink to the indignity of struggling against him, suffering his touch steadfastly. Her frenzied anger became a dreadful frigid calm. She waited.

Gradually, his hand loosened, then fell away. "All right." He took a single step backward and Christen thought she would be burned by the lash of his stormy glare even as he retreated. "I won't touch you again."

Christen nodded, accepting his words as a promise. "What do you want, Zachary? Why are you here?"

"I've told you."

"There's more to it than Nathan. What game are you playing?"

"No game."

Studying him, Christen saw the hard assurance of a man who knew what he wanted and would not be afraid to take it. It made no sense that he would come for her after five years. But, if he wanted her, in hatred, for revenge, or for reasons she had yet to understand, it would not be a game. It would be a battle and the hard, fierce look of him promised no quarter.

"All right, no game." She lifted a querying brow. "No rules?"

"None."

Christen held his stare for a moment longer. "One."

"One," Zachary agreed. He crossed his arms over his chest. The gold chain and its emblem winked in the refracted light reminding Christen that they were alone and Zachary was a magnificent man.

"No matter what happens between us, Nathan won't be hurt."

"He's my friend. I won't hurt him. You have my word."

Christen bowed her head, looking down at her hands folded one inside the other. Once she had been Zachary's friend. Until they had stepped beyond the bonds of friendship and destroyed everything. Flinging back her head she looked directly at him. "So be it," she murmured her agreement.

The gauntlet had been thrown, the challenge made. There was no need for discussion. She knew there would be unspoken rules in this seemingly ruleless encounter. They were professionals and would conduct themselves as such in the clinic. In one way or another Medicine had been salvation for each of them. In their oath they accepted a commitment and the burden of a trust neither would violate.

Christen looked away. Beyond the darkened window a maple whispered in a rising breeze. Its leaves had grown bright and brittle, losing the succulence of rich, pale green. Soon they would carpet the lawn. Bare limbs would reach like black shadows toward the sky.

Winter, stark, graceful, beautiful, her favorite season. There was honesty in its unadorned world and peace in its deep, silent nights. But not this year. This year the nights held no promise of peace.

"So be it." She repeated with her head bowed in thought.

"Christen?" He touched her shoulder, realized he had already broken his promise and jerked his hand away. But not before the weight of it on her rigid shoulder, the heat of it against her flesh, drew her from her reverie.

"It's late." She smiled wryly. "Or should I say early? Nathan will rise with the rooster. That hasn't changed. I'd like to breakfast with him. It might be the last for a long time."

"This thing with his lungs is serious but not life threatening, Christen. He won't be gone forever."

"*If* he leaves the mountain.'"

"He must."

"Then it's settled."

"Hasn't it been?"

"Yes." Shrugging, she realized that the exhilaration of her night flight had been snuffed out, its surge of adrenaline dissipated, sapping the little reserve she'd had left. Tension drew her body like a bowstring. Her eyes were dry and gritty. She desperately needed to sleep.

She had taken one tottering step when Zachary's fingers clamped about her wrist like an iron shackle. "Good God, woman! Just what have you done to yourself?" he demanded, his hold tightening painfully when she would have slipped free. "You're so exhausted you can hardly stand."

"I've been tired before. I will be again. This gracious little episode hasn't been exactly restful." Peeling his fingers one by one from her wrist she lifted his hand and dropped it away from her. "Good night, Zachary."

He made no other effort to touch her as she slipped by him and crossed to the door. "I'll be leaving in the morning," he said as she turned the knob.

She spun to face him, her hands behind her, leaning against the door for support. "Leaving?"

"I have some things to do in the city. Some loose ends to tie up." He waited for a comment. When she offered none he continued, "I didn't know...I wasn't sure...I left...a matter unresolved."

"Serious?"

"It could be."

"Then perhaps you should stay in the city and attend to this...ah...matter."

"No!"

"Someone else could be found to take your place here. We have a while before the bitter cold weather sets in. Nathan would be all right until then."

"I'm your partner for the next six months. Better get used to it. Better get used to me. There'll be no one else."

"That sounded like a threat."

"No threat. A promise."

"It needn't be. Once Nathan has made the transition to Arizona, or wherever, you can leave. I can manage alone."

"As you have today? Even with the little help Nathan could give you, you're beat. Forget it, Christen. I'll be here for the duration."

"Can you? Once you thought this was the end of the world, that I was destroying my life by coming home to work. Even before we...before I left, we quarreled for days if I hinted that I wanted to practice in Laurenceville. You're a creature of the city. Can you endure six months here in a virtual wilderness?''

"I'll survive."

A smile ghosted over her face as she saw a small glimmer of hope for her life as she knew it. Perhaps his struggles to survive would surpass his need to play the game that was not a game. The thought struck a dim light in the darkness of the coming winter.

"We shall see, shan't we?" She opened the door and stepped through it. "Good night, Zachary."

"Wait!"

She turned back wearily, anxious to be gone while some bit of her reserve remained. "It's almost morning. We'll have plenty of time in the next six months for discussion."

"One question."

"All right. One."

"Do I frighten you, Christen?"

She looked at him for an interminable time before replying quietly, "No, Zachary, you don't frighten me. Not any more."

It was true. She felt no fear of Zachary. Not as a physical man, and not alone. It was only together that they were volatile. If she acted sensibly he would be no more dangerous than she. This time she would not retreat.

"Good night, Dr. Steele," she said softly. "Get your rest. I have a feeling you'll need it. Oh, one more thing. When you come back, bring your flannel undies. You'll need them, too."

The door closed behind her and Zachary was left staring into the empty silence, wondering. Had he won the first round, or had she?

Four

Knock, knock."

"Come in, Gin." Christen looked up from the report she was reading. "Ready to go home?"

"Yup." Ginny Lowe tossed a towel over the shoulder of her nurse's uniform. "About time, too. My family must think I've skipped the country."

"Sorry." Christen grimaced. "It has been a long day and a longer week. I thought with Zachary here things would go smoother."

"Who said anything about not being smoother? Our trouble is there's more work. Half the women in the county who've been neglecting physicals have suddenly decided they shouldn't delay any longer."

"It's good they've had a change of heart, don't you think?" Christen pushed back from her desk barely containing a laugh. She knew what was coming.

"Change of heart, hah! Trying to catch a glimpse of Mr. Gorgeous is more like it."

"Mr. Gorgeous? Is that what you call him?"

"Among other things."

"Ginny, is there a problem?"

"No problem. He's been here three weeks and he's wonderful. I keep waiting for you to notice."

"No, no, and again, no!" Christen wagged a finger at her. "This clinic is hectic enough without matchmaking." The reprimand was affectionately given, for Ginny Lowe was a wonderful contradiction. At forty-six she was sleek and smooth, but beneath a strikingly sophisticated exterior lay a boundless energy, a constantly seeking mind, and motherly heart.

"Christen, if you insist on burying yourself in this backwater town, the least you could do is take advantage of opportunities that drop in your lap."

Christen laughed aloud. Folding her hands in her lap she said with mock innocence, "I recall a stunning blonde who passed up a future as a dancer for this backwater town."

"And a husband, and kids, and good schools, and clean air," Ginny drawled. "But the operative word is family."

"I have a family, Gin."

"Sure." Ginny leaned against the wall and propped one foot in front of the other. "You have your mother, the beautiful Elise Laurence, who's off somewhere spending the money she inherited from your dad's estate and chasing the latest in a series of young lovers. And let's not forget that when you were fifteen she tossed you out of the Laurence mansion to keep her third sweet young thing—or was he her fourth—away from you."

"I have Nathan," Christen said softly.

"Who is seventy-seven years old, and failing fast." Ginny's kind heart got the best of her matchmaking zeal.

"Darn it!" she said, using the strongest expletive Christen had ever heard her utter. "Chris, I'm sorry. I don't mean to hurt you. I know your experience with that slimy so-and-so when you were fifteen was awful. I know there was someone when you were away in residency. I know that losing Greg was terrible. You haven't exactly been lucky in love. But, my dear friend, you can't give up. Nothing is as destructive as loneliness."

"I'm not lonely. I haven't the time."

"Ha!" Ginny snorted indelicately. "Is that what you tell yourself when you're lying alone in that huge four-poster?"

"To be honest, I don't tell myself anything. I sleep."

"Honey, I'm here to tell you, there's better things to do in a bed than sleep. The product isn't half shabby either."

Christen thought of the five young sons who had arrived like clockwork until Albert Lowe teasingly pleaded age and exhaustion, and seriously noted a straining budget. "All right, Gin."

"All right?" Ginny shrugged away from the door, an incredulous smile on her face.

"Sure." Christen nodded. "As soon as ski season begins, I'll catch myself one of those hotdoggers. If I can convince him that I can keep him warmer than his skis we'll settle down and begin to make dozens of little skiers."

"Yuck!" Gin shook her head in disgust. "I give up."

"Good. Now go home to your family." She paused then added, "You know, one more boy and you would've had a substitute for your basketball team."

"Umm hmm." Ginny grinned as she prepared for one last zinger. "Except I foolishly waited too long, didn't I?" Before Christen could answer she reached into her pocket and drew out an envelope. "Here, I have a surprise for you. Came in the morning mail, but I thought it would be a nice lift for your lonely evening."

"Go!" Christen laughed as she eagerly picked up the letter from Nathan.

"By the way. Zack, or Zachary as you call him, left his car for you. He took the truck up to Sadie Greenway's cabin. I gave him directions."

"Good grief! You know she won't see him."

"Sure she will."

"Don't forget, he's only been here three weeks. I'd been here a year before she let me check her."

"Not the same thing at all. You were a sweet young twit, too wet behind the ears to know what you were doing—Sadie's words, not mine. Zack's a magnificent hunk of man—my words this time."

"Sadie's ninety years old."

"But she ain't blind, like some people I know," Ginny drawled.

"Go home, Gin."

"Going. Just one more thing."

Sighing, Christen laid down the treasured letter. "I should have known."

"It's a long, rough trip to Sadie's."

"We both know that quite well."

"The road will jolt his spine clear out the top of his head."

"Probably. So?"

"So, when he gets in, why don't you lock Bell in her room, take the phone off the hook, light the fire, light a candle, open a bottle of wine, and then..."

"Yes?" With a quirk of her lips, Christen waited.

"Get naked and give him a good massage," Ginny blurted.

"You're fired, Gin."

"I know." Grinning, Ginny wagged her fingers in an exaggerated pantomime of goodbye. "See you tomorrow."

"Tomorrow." Christen said as the laughter that threatened spilled over.

"Hello. Anybody home? Bell?" Christen called as she let herself in the front door. The house was eerily quiet. Normally there would be sounds and scents of Bell's dinner preparations. Zachary wouldn't be home, of course. It was far too soon for his journey to Sadie's to be done.

"Strange," Christen said under her breath as she moved toward the kitchen. Passing by the study door, she saw that a fire had been laid, needing only the strike of a match to burst into flames. A small table sat before the hearth, with a vase of fall flowers from Nathan's garden in its center. The kitchen beyond was empty. A long note was tucked under a magnet in the center of the refrigerator door.

"Chris, I'm sure you've forgotten," Christen read. "This is the weekend I promised to help Hunter. You have probably also forgotten that his latest commission could hinge on the presentations he plans for his dinner guests. Not to worry, you won't starve—not that you'd notice. A casserole and salad in the fridge for this evening. Steaks for Saturday. Below follows a rather detailed instruction on how to proceed—which you will probably not read. In any case, have fun. See you Sunday. Bell."

Taking the note down as she opened the door, Christen discovered the casserole and salad exactly as Bell promised. It was past seven, Zachary shouldn't be much longer. After putting the casserole to bake in the oven, she left the kitchen.

She took longer in the bath than usual, then her freshly washed hair was unruly and required an inordinate time to tame. The first blouse she slipped into popped a button, the second looked and felt wrong. Finally she chose muted rose lounging pants and a long tailored shirt of a paler color. The silky fabric was deliciously elegant as it clung and swayed about her.

"Good grief!" she set a flagon of perfume down with a thud. "What am I doing? Zachary and I are having dinner alone. Why am I dressing like this? Ginny's nonsense must have taken root when I wasn't looking." Shaking her head she returned to her closet to make another selection. "Jeans and a sweatshirt should do."

She was just taking the fresh pair of jeans from a hanger when a knock rattled her door.

"Are you decent, Christen?"

Whirling, she dropped the jeans in a heap at her feet. "Zachary," she said feeling foolishly guilty, like a child caught playing dress-up. "I didn't hear you come in."

"Obviously."

"How was your trip?"

"My trip was . . . Look, Christen, do we have to have this conversation through the door?"

"Oh. Sorry." She looked at shimmering rose slacks. Definitely not what she'd intended he would see her in, but there was no help for it now. "Coming," she called, crossing the room.

When the door swung open Zachary was leaning against its frame. His shirt was open at the neck, the sleeves rolled back. He was tanned, disheveled and covered with dust. "This," he gestured at his grimy clothing, "is how my trip went."

Christen burst out laughing at his droll expression. "You found the road to Sadie's."

"And every pothole along the way."

"You'll want a shower before dinner. Oh dear." She clapped her hand to her forehead. "The casserole! I forgot!"

"That's why I stopped by," Zachary said. "To tell you I turned down the oven temperature. Enough to give me time to remove a layer or two of this dirt." He turned his gaze to her, his sapphire eyes sweeping her figure, accentuated rather than disguised by flowing rose silk.

She wore no jewelry, and the slight tinge of color in her cheeks had nothing to do with makeup. At thirty-three, six years and a lifetime of experience younger than he, she still looked as deceptively innocent and unspoiled as a virgin. "Maybe I should've turned the temperature lower and given myself time for a little more polish. I didn't expect you to be quite so nicely turned out."

"Oh," Christen's hands went self-consciously to her throat. "This?" She looked down. "Uh, it's new. I was trying it on, checking for any needed alterations." She gestured awkwardly toward the crumple of blue denim. "I was just going to slip into jeans."

"Don't," he said quickly, his intense gaze seeking out the hidden silhouette of her body, probing the rounded line of her breasts, lingering on the shadowed cleft bared by the deep cut of her blouse. "You look lovely," he murmured. "Far too lovely to change."

She heard the low, intimate rasp in his voice and felt it pulsate in the deep core of herself. Tugging absently at a button she said, "There's dinner to be done. The salad . . . I . . . I should change."

"No!" He clasped her wrist, his long fingers closing about it, the back of his hand brushing against the swell of her breasts. For a long, silent moment he said nothing. The same intensity that had explored the hidden secrets of her body swept lazily over her bright chestnut hair. Rich, red-brown like cinnamon, the fruit of an exotic laurel tree.

She wore it back from her forehead, the ends brushing her shoulders. There was no curl, no artifice, the glorious weight of it its adornment. Gleaming like burnished copper, it was made darker by the creamy translucence of her skin. Beneath winged brows her heavily fringed eyes were pure green fire. "I like to look at you," he said huskily as his gaze slid boldly down the graceful column of her throat, touching with a lover's delight on the gentle rise and fall of her breasts.

"You aren't afraid of me," he reminded her in a soft-voiced challenge. "And why should you be? With Bell's casserole to quench my hunger, and an angel to please my eye, is there more I could dare ask?"

Lifting her fingers to his lips he kissed them lightly, smiling at her through dark, gold-tipped lashes. She wanted to draw her hand from his and escape the knowledge she saw in those mesmerizing eyes. Denial of her hunger for his touch was a tiny whisper, echoing through the dark canyons of her mind.

"We've worked and lived together for three weeks and this will be our first dinner alone. We should make it an occasion." He released her hand and stepped away. Bowing slightly, he said softly, "Dr. Laurence, would you do me the honor of dining with me in the privacy of our home?"

He was teasing her, but beneath it lay a promise of something far more dangerous than dinner alone. *He* was danger, but no matter. Suddenly she wanted to banish from her mind that faint warning voice and risk what he offered. She wanted to spend an evening with a man who looked at her as if she were beautiful and desirable. No! she admitted with raw honesty. She wanted to spend the evening with *Zachary* and have him look at her with desire.

She had likened this madness to dancing in flames. Now she knew she wanted to dance and risk the burn. "I'd be delighted to have dinner with you, Dr. Steele," she heard herself say in a voice she hardly recognized as her own.

A gleam of triumph shone in his eyes, but in her reckless mood she didn't care. "Thirty minutes?" he asked.

"Of course."

Leaving her all dressed up in her finery, he nodded curtly and turned away without a backward glance.

Why would he say more? she wondered as the black, bitter truths of reality crept into her mind. He'd gotten what he wanted with a persuasive look and a smile and dismissed her for now. The little resistance she'd offered had melted as in an inferno. What would she do when he wanted more? If she couldn't deny him, would she become the prize of the conqueror to be used and discarded?

The wild magic of the moment when he looked at her was shattered. She had seen him in the rose-colored reflection of her garments and for a mad instant forgot the hurt and the years that separated them. They could never be as they were before. Recalling the gleam of sardonic triumph that had glinted in his eyes, she was shamed by her weakness. She had played into his hands like a simpering fool. One little compliment and he'd had her slavering at his feet. Was he laughing at his easy conquest?

Christen slammed the door in mute despair. Leaning against it, she struggled to calm the rising storm of her anger. "A smile and a compliment and I'm no better than Elise," she said bitterly. "What a fool I am." Tearing at the buttons of her shirt she crossed again to the closet, sweeping the jeans from the floor. She had shrugged half out of her shirt when she stopped.

"No!" There was a brittle edge in the word. "Two can play this game." Pulling the shirt back over her naked breasts, she buttoned it, leaving the top carelessly undone. At the mirror she brushed her hair savagely, pulling back one side and pinning it with the silk flower that matched her slacks. A dot of perfume to her wrists, one behind each ear and a long glissade between her breasts, and her preparations were complete.

A final glimpse in the mirror and one more button flicked from its mooring drew a sober promise from her. "No rules, Zachary."

Thirty minutes later she was sitting before a dancing fire. The salad was tossed. The casserole waited in its chafing dish. The candles were lit and a bottle of wine rested in a frosty bucket of ice. Christen sipped from her tall glass, stared into the flames, and waited.

Her day had been long, and anger made inroads on her strength. The room was warm, easing the chill from her heart. The flames of the fire were bright, soothing and hypnotic. She must have dozed off for the next thing she knew was that Zachary had taken the glass from her hand.

He was crouched before her, the fire behind him turning his white-gold hair the color of sunset. When he stood, looking down at her silently, she saw he had, indeed, dressed for dinner. The black, single-breasted jacket of a rough but elegant fabric stopped short of his hips, leaving the lean line of his corded thighs unfettered and broadening his shoulders incredibly in contrast. The white, tucked shirt and satin band at his waist might be effete on another man, but clothed in any fashion, Zachary was far too virile to be less than totally male.

"Hi, sleepyhead," he said in a low voice as he set the glass aside. "Tough day at the office?"

Befuddled by sleep and by the tenderness she heard in him, Christen stared at him, eyes wide and unguarded.

"I hope that sweet, unfocused look is for me. Though why someone as sexy as you would give a second glance to a battered old war-horse like me is a mystery."

"You're beautiful, Zachary," she blurted and the words had the shock of a pail of ice thrown in her face. She was playing the fool again.

Zachary laughed. "No one's ever accused me of being beautiful before." Taking her hand he helped her from the couch. "I'm starved. That's what I am."

He led her to the table and seated her. When he would have replenished her glass from the wine bottle, Christen covered its rim with her palm. "The wine is for you."

Lazily he picked up her glass and drank from it. A look of surprise crossed his features as the clear, effervescent liquid touched his lips. "Sparkling grape juice."

"I drink very little. I never know when there might be a call."

"I see." He set down her glass and picked up his own, discovering the juice bottle in a second bucket nearby. "Then we'll both keep our wits about us tonight." Filling his glass he lifted it high. "To good companions."

Zachary proved a good dinner companion. His conversation was varied and interesting and kept her constantly on her toes. It had been so long since she'd had dinner alone with an attractive man who devoted himself solely to her wishes, she found herself slipping again under his spell, forgetting the challenge, the ruleless game.

A man like Zachary was lethal for a lonely woman, but she threw caution to the wind and listened raptly to his conversation, laughing softly at his humor. Her guard was down. The juice they drank became the headiest wine. The night took on a glow as she leaned nearer, hanging on every word, responding to the heavy lidded gaze that flicked over the open buttons on her blouse. Clutching at a waning sense of self-preservation, she pushed back her glass commanding, "Tell me about yourself."

"You know all there is to know, Christen."

"Not really. We never found time to talk."

"We didn't, did we?" An oddly surprised look crossed his face. "We thought we knew each other, though." Without waiting to see if the barb hit home he continued. "I suppose too late is better than never at all. What would you like to know?"

"Everything."

"That's a tall order." Sliding back his chair he stood. With his hands in his pockets he looked about him. The ceilings were high, built to accommodate furniture that was antique today. The room was always gracious and cheerful. By day it was bright with filtered sunlight, by night shadowed, restful. A cluster of comfortable chairs was gathered beyond the fireplace where a small fire still blazed. The fragrance of fresh flowers perfumed the air, and a well-stocked bar tempted one's tastes.

The room was a testament for the mastery of the eighteenth-century craftsman. Solid cherry, hand-sanded, hand-rubbed, until it glowed with the depth of a rich patina; brass, heavy, detailed and polished to a bright, burnished glow; rich, butter-soft leather and fabrics as bright and pleasant as the sun. The mark of distinction, of history and heritage. The banner of success. This room was what his life had been about.

"Do you know how fortunate you were to grow up in a home like this?" he asked, an unintentional roughness in the question.

Christen hadn't grown up in "a home like this" as he referred to it, but she wanted to hear Zachary's story—not tell hers. "Nathan and Bell have a talent for making a home comfortable."

"Where I grew up is so foreign to this it might have been another country, another continent. Hell! Another planet. There was no gentility in that life. My father deserted me for

places unknown, my mother for the bottle. My grandmother tried, but she was old, and her English poor. I was
in the streets by the time I was twelve. Working the shrimp
boats and fishing trawlers off Brighton when I could cajole
a berth and if not, sleeping where I could, eating when and
if I could. To survive I learned to be quick with my hands
and quicker with my fists. On the boats I learned to love the
sea and grew strong. In the chaos of the alleys I became an
adept brawler, as quick with my wit as I was with an accomplished left hook. If that can be considered an accom-
plishment.''

"You did what was needed. There's no shame in that.''
He rewarded her with a crooked, half-smile and she fell silent, waiting.

"At grandmother's insistence I stayed in school. Sporad-
ically, between working the boats or sneaking a rare sail, but
enough that some do-gooder discovered there was a brain
beneath my wild mop of hair. At first it wasn't good news.
It was one more complication.''

Christen nodded. She did not understand but dared not
interrupt to question.

Forgetting his decision to drink as she did, Zachary
walked to the bar, poured a splash of whiskey in a heavy
crystal glass and dropped in an ice cube. As he sipped it,
feeling it bite and curl through him like smoke, he could
look back and see the irony that the very intelligence that set
him apart had also drawn him into skirmishes that left their
share of scars. "From the moment a pompous teacher
pointed a finger at me and damned me for my poor grades
I was marked. If I acted intelligently I was resented. If I
didn't it was worse. A no-win situation with all avenues
leading to the same end.''

"But you beat the odds," she said almost to herself.
Thinking of the street fighter's swagger, the toughness, and

that odd, gentle mixture of old world charm, she could see how he was already set apart. His intelligence would in a strange way be another burden. No wonder he had built a barrier about himself, never speaking of his past, nor letting anyone into his life.

Except me, she thought with an odd lift of pride. Though they had once been good friends, he rarely spoke of his past, nor she of hers. Then, in a mad, exhilarated moment, that special time only those who had fought death and disease and won could know, he had taken her into his arms. For that little time they shared something that shattered the guarded barriers their hurts had constructed. But the total honesty of complete sharing demanded an unreserved surrender. One that threatened the premises on which she had built her life and, in fear of her own weakness, she fled.

She hadn't realized the gift he'd offered her, nor the pain she caused when she had thrown it away. Now, aching inside as she hadn't known she could, Christen lifted her eyes to his. "It did end," she said with an odd wistfulness in her voice.

A savage anger glinted in his eyes. The heat of it impaled her until he shrugged and looked away. In a husky rasp he said, "Don't you know, that some things never end, Christen?"

"And some things do." She answered gently as she tried not to flinch under the velvet lash of his words. "You left the streets behind you."

His eyes narrowed in unwilling admiration for the skillful parry of her thrust. He nodded and touched an imaginary hat brim as if to say, touché. "Yes, I did," he agreed with a ghost of a smile on his face. "But not without my share of lumps. I was undirected and misdirected, until the day I found a medical book spilled from a garbage can.

"I have no idea how it came to be there. It was tattered and torn, but far more intriguing than the other books I scrounged. In it I discovered a new world. For the first time I was glad for my so-called intelligence. There was escape from the squalor of the city and medicine would be mine."

"You never wavered in your ambition." She watched him as he lovingly traced a finger over one of the leather-bound volumes that filled Nathan's library, thinking of the sadness of a child whose only ray of hope had come in the form of a book found in Brighton's refuse.

"It wasn't that simple." He left the bookshelves and at the bar poured himself another whiskey. "First came Vietnam and there my sole ambition was to survive."

"Were you an officer?"

"Hardly." His bark of laughter was harsh and humorless. "I was a foot soldier. My job was to kill and not be killed. I'd never had friends. In Nam I didn't want any."

Better not to. It would hurt too badly when they died. The thought stabbed at Christen's mind.

"Then Jacobi came, with his pockets stuffed with bandages and syringes and ampules. 'Might lose my pack, but never my pockets,' he said. He was a good kid with a big grin no one could resist."

And Zachary had found his first real friend whether he wanted him or not. Christen's heart contracted into a cold lump as she visualized two young men who were really little more than children. One lonely and aloof, already wounded by the wars of the street. The other perhaps open and warm, drawn by a need to salve the invisible wounds. There was a sting of tears in her eyes as she listened with a growing dread to the rest of the story.

"I worked with him when I could, using what I'd learned from the book." He lifted the whiskey to his lips before he realized his hand was trembling so badly he couldn't drink.

He set the glass on a table with such force the amber liquid splattered on his wrist. He stared down at his saturated hands half expecting that they would be crimson. As they had been the day Jacobi died.

Jerkily, he moved to the fire, letting its warmth ease the sudden chill that touched him. He rarely thought of Jacobi now, yet every day of his life was a tribute to the young medic. Jacobi's life and his death had opened up a new horizon for a younger, greener kid who was more an idealist than he would admit.

"Jacobi died," Christen murmured, gently voicing the hated phrase for him. Taking that small burden from him.

"Yes." Zachary sighed heavily and stared stonily into the flames for so long she thought his story would end there.

The fire crackled. A small flame danced merrily the length of a dwindling log and was snuffed out. Trapped in a silence that weighed heavily on him, Zachary seemed to have forgotten that Christen was there. Beyond the door, the grandfather clock chimed a portion of the hour. Slowly, like a huge bear waking from winter's sleep, he shrugged.

"He was going to a wounded soldier when he stepped on a mine." There was a weariness in Zachary, and a knowledge that made young men old before their time. "He was a good man. He deserved better. Because of Jacobi, I discovered I wanted to preserve life, not take it."

For the first time, Christen understood the anger and passion she had seen in him as a resident. She could even understand his fury when he felt she was betraying her talent. A nagging idea that had plagued her subconscious for weeks coalesced into thought. Something had been subtly wrong about Zachary. Now she saw it clearly. He was still good at his work, his patients loved him, but the zeal, the tremendous drive that had set him apart, had died. He was a solitary man who had somehow lost touch with the most important thing in his life, his work.

The sabbatical! Scheduled *before* Nathan's offer of work for six months. She hadn't questioned its purpose. Had Zachary taken it needing more than a rest? In the flickering firelight there was strength in his handsome chiseled features, but in this unguarded moment, she saw sadness more profound than grief. In a voice strained with the ache of tears she dared not shed, she said softly, "I had Greg, you had Jacobi. They sound very much alike."

"And they're both dead." Zachary hit the mantle with a massive fist. With his head bowed he stared again into the embers of the fire. Only their red glow lit the room for the candle had long since gutted and died. "Dance with me." He spun to face her with his arms outstretched. "Dance with me and forget."

Music from the radio, muted, and until now unnoticed, drifted to her in a mellow melody. His look dared her to refuse, but Christen had no intention of refusing. He was no longer a threat. He was a man who had been lonely all his life and had lost his only friend. A man whose special gift had grown tarnished. He was hurting and she wouldn't deny him any more than she would a patient who was sick and in pain.

Rising gracefully, she moved into his arms. At first he only held her, his arms about her waist, the strong line of his powerful thighs against hers. Then gradually he began to sway, bringing her closer, the heat of her body the only surcease for the haunting chill of his lost friend's grave.

His steps were slow, with no pattern, yet not difficult to follow. The pressure of his hand at the curve of her waist, gentle but commanding, was her guide. The silk of her blouse caught in the rough texture of his jacket, sliding, caressing her bare breasts as he might have. A quaking excitement stirred in her and her hand trembled at his nape.

"Easy," he soothed. "Don't think of anything. Just listen. Music is like sailing, it soothes the hurt."

His hand slid beneath her shirt, his rough fingers burning into her flesh. His lips touched her temple, his golden lashes tangling in her hair. She knew she should move away, establish a sense of decorum between them, but she hadn't the strength. They circled the room. Once, twice. Shadows deepened as the fire died to a dull red-gray. The cold crept in, the music stopped. Still he danced.

"Zachary." She murmured as his lips moved silently against the fragile curve of her temple, his warm breath teasing her hair. "It's late."

On cue the clock in the hall boomed once. Putting her from him he held her at arm's length, his hands gripping her arms. There was cold between them where once their bodies had shared warmth. His eyes were hooded and unreadable in the near darkness. His palms stroked up her arms to her shoulders, fingers twining in her hair. "There's fire in your hair, did you know that?" He asked in a hoarse, growling mutter. "Did you know that's what I remembered most about you? How it gleamed like rippling fire on the pillow."

He was rambling. The whiskey talked and needed no answer. Christen stood patiently under his hands.

"You're a dangerous woman. I wanted to forget, but you make me forget too much." He leaned nearer. His mouth brushed hers lightly, tentatively, moved away then returned. "Soft," he growled against her lips. "So soft."

Christen turned her face away. He used it as an opportunity to capture her earlobe in his mouth, touching the hollow beneath it with his tongue. Her breath was a single gasp as she cried, "Stop, Zachary. You don't know what you're doing."

He caught her chin in his hand, turning her face to him. "I know exactly what I'm doing."

His mouth closed over hers, silencing her protest before it was born. His lips were soft, parting hers with a gentle insistence. His tongue caressed the velvet softness of her flesh, his hand cupped her naked breast teasing its nipple to the sweet pain of arousal. For a moment she clung to him, her fingers threading through the fine gold of his hair, bringing his mouth hard against her own as her tongue met his. There was a madness in her that wanted more.

His lips slid down the graceful arch of her neck, lingering at the hollow of her throat before seeking the soft, creamy swell of her breasts. "No rules," he muttered, parting her blouse, the light growth of his beard scratching the tender bud of a nipple he exposed.

No rules.

She had agreed, but now she was afraid. Not of Zachary, even in his slightly drunken state and here with him alone in the big rambling house. She was more afraid of herself and what she might incite in him. "Wait." She nearly strangled on the word as his mouth closed over a nipple, his suckling sending splinters of lightning through her. Her legs almost betrayed her then, but the small voice of her sanity warned disaster. "Don't, Zachary."

"Christen." His warm breath cooled the moist tip of her breast. "Don't tell me no."

Her fingers wound tighter in his hair. "Stop!" She cried in panic. "You don't know what you're doing."

He muttered a guttural expletive, releasing her so suddenly she would have fallen but for the hand that caught at her shoulder steadying her. His face was a harsh, shadowed mask. "I was doing exactly what you wanted." A cold look flicked over her bare breast, heaving beneath the opened rose silk. "Where I come from, lady, when you dress for the role, you play the part. You can't tell a man you want him with every look and not expect trouble. Dammit!" He loosened his hold and left her swaying on her feet. "Stop playing the tease. Cover yourself."

Christen stared numbly at him. Her eyes nearly black with shock, held the haunted look of a small wounded animal.

Zachary closed his eyes, sparing himself the sight of her. Then, with a heavy sigh and a muttered expletive of a milder nature his eyelids fluttered and opened. Silently and carefully he began to close the buttons of her blouse. At the last, his task complete, he muttered hoarsely. "I won't apologize. I'm not sure I could."

Turning on his heel he left her, mute and trembling, and bewildered.

Five

"Another week. Done! Finished! Kaput! Thank God!"
Christen dropped a chart on Ginny's desk. With thumb and
forefinger she massaged her temples. "Has Friday always
been such a great distance from Monday?"

Ginny stood, picked up the chart, flipped through the files
and slid it into its proper slot. "Tough week, huh."

"Murder."

"Maybe it wouldn't be so bad if you got a little rest in
between." She looked pointedly at the faint smudges beneath the younger woman's eyes. "A little sleep could cure
what ails you."

"I've had a lot on my mind, and Lucy Foster is on a
tear."

"Let me guess," Ginny said drolly. "She's watching Dr.
Kildare reruns again. And, about one in the a.m. when all
good people should be sleeping, and she's finished her first

pint of the evening, your phone rings. Presto! She has the latest symptoms. What was it last night? Jungle rot?"

"Almost. And it was Ben Casey."

"What she has is brain rot from booze, and hypochondria from having too little to occupy her time."

"I think the calls are truly cries for help, Ginny. She can't quite bring herself to admit it."

"So you keep her pumped full of vitamins, and commiserate with each new set of symptoms into the wee hours of the morning."

"Keeping the channel open is far more important than a few hours sleep." Christen was inordinately grateful that Ginny had constructed such a plausible reason for her sleepless nights. She felt a pang of guilt that Poor Lucy had taken the blame, but she wasn't ready for Ginny to know that it was thoughts of Zachary and what had passed between them that kept her tossing restlessly through the nights.

"At least you won't have to worry about her this weekend. The young medical Galahads from Brighton can deal with her."

"I'll write a note explaining Lucy. Have you pulled the charts they might have questions about?" Christen had never been quite so glad that once each month a team of Family Practice residents manned the clinic as part of an externship program.

"All done." Ginny gestured at a stack of charts and the notations on each. She grinned at Christen. "You have over forty-eight hours of total freedom. How are you and Mr. Gorgeous going to spend them?"

"I promised *Hunter* I'd spend a couple of days with him. He needs some preliminary sketches."

"A new project?"

"Umm humm. A bronze, commissioned by the husband of an historical romance writer. A surprise to celebrate her best-seller. Hunter only needs a few sketches. After that I'm going to sleep and eat, and read, and sit in his solarium basking in the winter sun."

"He still disappears once he catches the mood he wants?"

"Posing for Hunter is not as simple as it sounds. Sometimes I sit for hours hardly daring to breathe. But, yes, once he has the ideas he needs, he disappears."

"Must be tiresome. You're already worn out. Just this one time why don't you ask him to find another model?"

"Can't." Christen sighed softly, then smiled at her friend. "You know I've been the model for most of his work."

"His good luck charm."

"Maybe. This session might be rough though. Bell said this bronze was to be really special."

"The solarium sounds like heaven, at least."

"It will be."

"What about Dr. Zack?

Christen shrugged carelessly. "I suppose he'll go home to Brighton. It's been a month since he's been in the city. There must be things that need his attention. Perhaps he'll go sailing. He must miss it." She slipped open the clasp that held her hair tightly at her nape and dropped it in her pocket, a familiar signal that her day was done.

"Christen, there's one more patient."

"But I thought . . ."

"I let the rest of the staff leave. I thought it was best."

"Benjie?"

Ginny nodded. "Dr. Zack's in with him now. You were busy and he wanted to see the child."

"It doesn't matter. Nathan and I never considered a patient exclusively ours, I don't suppose Zachary and I should either." She hesitated, then asked quietly, "How bad is it?"

"Hopefully just a case of the sniffles. No temp, no sign of secondary infection."

"I hope you're right." A dull, aching sense of helplessness settled like a shroud over Christen's heart. Benjie, with his unruly shock of snow-white hair, and huge dark eyes, was one of her favorites. Three short years of life had brought him only illness and pain. In an age of great advances in the treatment of leukemia, nothing worked for Benjie. "Do you think Zachary would object if I sat in on the examination?"

"I suspect he'd appreciate it."

Christen touched Ginny's shoulder and smiled. "Call it a day. Zachary and I can manage from here." To forestall any argument she walked hurriedly away. At the closed door of an examining room she tapped lightly.

The knob rattled and the door swung open. Zachary filled the door, his shoulders startlingly broad in the lab coat he wore. A stethoscope, as battered as only an old favorite could be, dangled from his neck. Beyond him Benjie sat, pale and still, and quiet.

With one golden brow lifted in query, Zachary asked, "Is there something you need, Christen?"

No rancor in his voice, no harshness, only polite, professional courtesy. It had been the same at home on the rare occasions when they couldn't avoid each other. Zachary was the perfect gentleman, the perfect stranger, since the disturbing exchange last weekend. The pall of awkward quiet that fell between them in its aftermath had set Bell's head shaking in puzzlement more than once.

"I'd like to sit in on Benjie's examination."

"We've just finished."

"Then I'd like to say hello. Benjie's one of my favorite people."

"Of course." Still that perfect courtesy. But the veneer of cynical civility could not mask the savage cold in his gaze. He stepped aside to let her enter.

"Jill." She smiled a greeting and patted the mother's frail shoulder. Kneeling before the child she stroked his colorless cheek and murmured, "Hi, Benjie. How's it going? Not so good today, huh?" There was no answer, no smile, only wide, dark eyes that never left her face. She glanced down at the chart that lay on the examining table beside the child. "Dr. Steele says that there's nothing to worry about and that in a day or so you should feel better."

The sound of a heavy engine rattled unevenly across the parking lot, then settled into a coughing hum. "I think your granddad just drove up and he's waiting in the cold, so I'll say goodbye and let Dr. Steele speak with your mom." The stolid face did not change, the dark eyes never looked away as she rumpled his hair and touched his cheek before turning away.

"Ginny's gone," she said to Zachary, her voice strained. "If you'll lock up?"

He turned that cold look on her. She expected to feel the sting of it like stones of ice pounding her flesh. Instead the pale eyes darkened and the hard edge of his expression softened. As if by its own desire his hand lifted to her face, a gentle finger brushing a clinging, crystalline tear from her lashes. A breath caught harshly in his chest, his hand jerked away as if she were fire. There was a guttural savagery in the voice that rasped, "Go home. I'll see to the office."

It took all her strength to hold back the tears until she reached her car. But on the lonely drive to Hunter's, in the secret shadows of twilight, they coursed in silver paths down her face. She wept for a child who would never know the joy of a single pain-free day. She wept for a man whose dream had somehow gone astray. She wept for herself and did not understand why.

Christen stood utterly still, her head thrown back, a leather thong holding the loose cascade of her hair. At her moccasin-shod feet lay a bow and quiver of arrows. Only the slow rise and fall of her breasts beneath the tattered leather shirt she wore distinguished her from one of Hunter's more lifelike sculptures.

Beyond her the copper-skinned Cherokee sat, sketch pad and pens in hand, a frown on his face, a worried look in his eyes. Setting his work aside he said quietly, "This isn't going to work. I need War Woman, the Tuscarora maiden who will lead her people in battle. Instead I have a dear, but very distracted friend."

"Sorry. I can't seem to get the attitude."

"Any particular problem?"

"Benjie was in the clinic today."

"Any better?" Hunter asked.

"No, but no worse either."

"Still doesn't smile?"

"Never."

"Poor kid," Hunter muttered. "I know what seeing him does to you."

"I feel so helpless."

Hunter rose from his seat and crossed the room on silent feet. "Chris," he stroked her cheek with the roughened tip of one finger. "Benjie is part of the problem, but not all. Would you like to talk about him?"

"Him?"

"Dr. Zachary Steele, the man from your past. The lover from your past."

Christen made no effort to deny his observations. Hunter's artist's eye would not be fooled. "How..." she looked away from the dark well of his obsidian eyes. "How did you know?"

"You told me."

"I never..."

"It's in your face. In your eyes. Every look."

"No!"

"Honey, I've known you since you were six. I've been drawing you since we were sixteen." Framing her face between his huge hands he said gently, "I know this lovely face better than anyone else on earth. I see beyond the facade."

"Hunter, I—"

He cut her protests short. "For instance, I know you were never in love with Greg. Not before you went away to school, nor after you returned."

"You're wrong. I did love Greg."

"You loved him," Hunter agreed mildly. "But you weren't in love with him. There's a difference, Christen."

"I did. I was!"

"No. If you had been, you wouldn't have kept him waiting, hoping, for two years."

"I loved Greg. I just wasn't ready for marriage."

"It wasn't marriage you weren't ready for, Christen. It was fulfilling the marriage vows. Forsaking all others, making love with a man you didn't love."

"How could you know Greg and I were never lovers?"

"The same way I know that you and Steele were."

"My blasted face!"

"Your lovely face. Greg was comfortable, undemanding. Too comfortable. What I see when you look at Zachary Steele is a fierce passion that burns all the hotter as you deny it."

"No man will wear my scalp on his belt!" Christen muttered.

"No man but Zachary Steele. He's counted that coup."

"I won't grovel for any man, Hunter." There was a look on her face that grimly transcended anger. "I promised myself a long time ago that I never would."

"Loving isn't groveling, Chris."

"Isn't it?"

"Love is a lot of things, but it's nothing to fear."

"You're quite the expert these days, aren't you? So tell me, my fearless Solomon, where is the woman in your life?" Christen saw the sudden tightening of his proud features, the glitter in his eyes. Ignoring it, she lashed out, "One disastrous affair and you withdraw. That's it! No more entanglements. Why is it that it was right for you but not for me?"

"Susan wanted the thrill of making love with a savage, but not the ignominy of being married to a stupid half-breed. Susan taught me a valuable lesson."

"Just as my mother and her lovers taught me. You don't want any part of Susan's world anymore than I do of my mother's." Shaking back her hair in a defiant gesture Christen muttered, "I will *not* be like my mother. I will *never* be a slave to love."

"That's it!" Hunter grabbed her shoulders, his fingers digging into her flesh. "Don't move, don't even breathe." He hurried to his sketch pad. In broad sweeping strokes he began to draw, the tight look of anger gone from him as he lost himself in his task.

Christen stood obediently, not even daring a glance at the small clock that normally served to remind both artist and model of carefully scheduled breaks. Tonight Hunter seemed not to hear its soft buzz. Partly in contrition for her cruel insult, partly because she always hated disturbing him when he was working so intensely, she posed far longer than was comfortable. Finally as her body grew numb and leaden she cried out, "Hunter! Please! No more."

Hunter looked up, satisfaction on his features, his gaze unfocused. Christen knew he no longer saw her. She had become War Woman, his creation.

"I have to move. My neck feels as if someone hit it with a sledgehammer, and my right arm ceased to exist an hour ago."

"Christen?" Hunter's effort to draw himself from his work was almost palpable. Glancing vaguely at the tiny timepiece he muttered, "Good grief! It's been hours. Sorry, honey. Relax."

Shrugging her shoulders and flexing the fingers of her deadened hand she asked, "Good?"

"Better than good. Perfect! And you'll be happy to hear, it's all I should need for a while. Why don't you go on into the kitchen and have a bite to eat. Mother left her usual supply of prepared foods when she was here last weekend."

"What about you?"

"I'm fine. I just want to do a little more work in here. Some refinement of an idea."

Christen had seen the look on his face before. He would immerse himself in this project and not surface for days. Perhaps he would stop to eat, perhaps not.

"I could head on home," she suggested.

"No, I like knowing you're here."

Christen nodded. He sometimes needed her again, when a look or mood escaped him, but only rarely.

"Just make yourself comfortable. You know where everything is."

"Hunter," Christen caught at his sleeve. "Forgive me."

He looked down at her, a puzzled expression on his face. "For what?"

"For what I said about Susan."

"Don't apologize for admitting the truth, honey. Just be sure you do admit it."

"I don't know if I can."

Drawing her beneath the shelter of his arm, he kissed her forehead. "Yes, you can. Look." He picked up a sketch. Christen barely recognized herself. Dressed in the rough clothing, with a proud look of defiance on her face, Hunter had made her far too beautiful. "War Woman," he said quietly. "A woman who can do anything."

"That's not me. I'm not that beautiful, nor that strong."

"I drew the strength and beauty I saw." He drew her closer with the familiar gentleness of an old friend. "I drew you, Christen."

"Well, well." A harsh voice cut like a knife through their quiet conversation. "Is this how you pose for the great artist, Christen?"

"Zachary!" Whirling from Hunter's embrace, Christen faced him. "What are you doing here?"

"Here?" Zachary looked about him. At the scattering of discarded drawings, at the revealing costume she wore. His gaze sliding over the loosened laces that exposed the full swell of her breast, down the length of a shapely leg revealed by the abbreviated skirt. "I knocked. When no one answered, I let myself in and followed my nose."

"I think Christen is asking what you're doing here, at my home." Hunter checked the small clock. "It's after midnight."

"Christen seemed upset over Benjie. I couldn't sleep for thinking she might need me. Bell gave me directions to your house." Zachary spoke to Hunter without taking his eyes from Christen, now he faced the larger man. "I see I was mistaken. Any comforting she might need, you can give her when you take her to bed. That is where the little scene I just interrupted is leading, isn't it?"

"Ste'tsi!" Hunter's harsh bark swept away Christen's shocked gasp.

"Does that gibberish mean you're not lovers?" Zachary drawled.

"That *gibberish* is Cherokee. I called you a child, Dr. Steele. To the Cherokee, a man who acts like a child is a fool and you're a damned fool."

Zachary's eyes narrowed, the grim line of his mouth quirked into a dangerous smile. "There was a time I would've taken you apart for that remark."

"There was a time I would've lifted your hair for that tone of voice, Dr. Steele."

"Do you think you could?"

"I don't think, I know."

"Christen must have told you, I grew up on the waterfront."

"And I grew up a breed."

"Point taken," Zachary nodded. He understood, for hadn't he been a bit of a half-breed himself? A misfit, with the challenges only a misfit could understand. "I think, under different circumstances, I could have liked you."

"What circumstances?" Christen cried out. She had watched these two very different, and yet very similar men, bristle and taunt one another long enough. "What the hell do you think you're talking about? Zachary, you walk in here like you own the place and accuse Hunter of being my lover, when it's none of your damn business if he is. And you," she rounded on Hunter, "You defend my honor like some buckskin knight. Even if we were lovers, I wouldn't need you to defend me to Zachary. Now, if you two pawing bulls will excuse me, I think I'll dress and go home."

"No, Christen, you can't," Hunter said.

"Ohh?" Christen lifted a sarcastic brow. "And why can I not?"

"It's been snowing for the last half hour. You'd never make it down without sliding into a ravine."

"How do you know?" Of course Hunter would know it was snowing. No matter how he buried himself in his work, certain intangible knowledge was always recorded deeply in his subconscious. "Your primitive intuition, Cherokee?"

Her calculated use of the name he wore proudly salved the intended sting of Zachary's insult. Hunter grinned. "My primitive nose, War Woman. I smelled it."

"You didn't say anything," she accused.

"I didn't know I knew, until just this minute. In any case, you were going to stay the weekend. I have strict orders from my mother to see that you do. And that you rest. I can get you down the mountain Sunday with the Cat."

"The Cat?" Zachary asked.

"The Caterpillar tractor I use to clear the drive on occasion. It also serves as an all-terrain vehicle at times." Hunter looked from Zachary to Christen and back again. "I don't know what you drove up this mountain, Mr. Street Fighter, but short of another Cat, it isn't going down."

Christen sighed in exasperation. "I'll start dinner."

"A midnight dinner?" Zachary drawled. "How romantic."

Christen ignored him, only the rippling of her jaw against her gritted teeth betrayed her. Evenly she continued, "I'll make up a bed for Zachary. Do you have a preference, Hunter?"

"I could share yours," Zachary taunted softly.

"Aren't you forgetting me, Dr. Steele?" Hunter intervened with what sounded suspiciously like a chuckle.

Christen looked from Zachary's darkening face to Hunter's, catching a look of dancing merriment on the Indian's handsome features. He was bedeviling Zachary. Giving him a taste of his own high-handedness. Almost choking on laughter that bubbled swiftly and unexpectedly, she said sweetly, "The blue room would be good, don't you think, darling? The one farthest from ours?"

"Certainly, the blue one. We wouldn't want to wake him with our, er, activities."

"Good. I'll see to it. Dinner should be ready in less than fifteen minutes." She left them to their own devices, the street brawler and the gentle savage.

Zachary watched her leave then turned to look into the depths of Hunter's unrelenting gaze. Blazing blue and smoldering black eyes met and held in a strange duel. Zachary was the first to look away. His chest heaved in a breath that might have been resignation or relief, not even he knew. After an interminable time he spoke in a hoarse voice. "You aren't her lover."

"No."

"You never have been."

"No."

"And I am a damned fool."

"A *ste'tsi*."

Zachary chuckled. "You don't mince words, do you?"

"No."

"Do you think Christen will forgive my stupidity?"

"That depends on Christen, and how apologetic you can be."

"I'm not good with apologies."

"You don't have to be good," Hunter observed wryly. "Just honest."

"Oh, I'm that all right."

"Are you?" Hunter straightened, he towered menacingly over Zachary. "I wouldn't want Christen to be misled by your purpose for being here."

"Here? Now? Or in Laurenceville?"

"Either. Both. I've seen this woman put her life back together twice now."

"Twice?"

"Twice," Hunter said tersely. "Because of you, once. And because of other, more complicated things once."

"Greg?"

"Greg was involved both times, but not in the way you think."

"How do you know what I think?"

"My primitive intuition, remember. And remember this, twice is enough for anyone to have to pick up the pieces and begin all over. If it happens again to Christen, you might regret it."

"Is that a threat?"

"It's a promise. I've never killed a man, but if you hurt her, I'd be tempted."

"I'll remember that."

"You do that. For now, why don't you join Christen in the kitchen, dinner must be almost ready."

"You won't be joining us?"

"No." Hunter picked up the sketches of Christen, studying them closely. "There's something I want to capture. Something I ..." His voice trailed away.

Zachary saw he'd been dismissed. Dismissed, but not forgotten. Never forgotten. "Good night, Hunter."

There was no answer, he hadn't expected one. Following the low sound of clattering crockery, he wandered to the kitchen. There he found Christen, an apron about her waist, setting the table for two.

"You expected me to brave the storm against Hunter's advice?" He gestured at the table, one setting short.

"I expected Hunter would retreat to his studio. The one out back, beyond the stream. He had that creative gleam in his eye. He does his preliminary work here in the house, but when he really gets into the mood of a piece he disappears into the studio."

"Funny." Zachary observed. "You saw creative genius in his eye. I saw mayhem."

"Mayhem!" Christen laughed. "There's not a gentler man alive than Hunter."

"You think so, huh?"

"I know so."

"I'll keep that in mind." Pulling a chair to the table he sat. "I'm hungrier than I thought I'd be."

Christen set a filled plate before him. "This is one of Bell's specialties. A late-night meal guaranteed not to weigh so heavily on the stomach that it precludes sleep. She knows Hunter's erratic work habits well."

"I don't suppose I should be surprised that you didn't prepare it. The pampered daughter of the renowned Laurences of Laurenceville would never need to learn to cook. Just how many servants did you have at your beck and call?"

"A few," she said coolly. "After my father died, what pampering the servants didn't do, Mother's lovers were always willing to supply. By the time I was fifteen, I never lacked for attention."

There was a grating note in her voice. Zachary looked up, surprising her, catching a look of pain before she could mask it. "What does that mean, Christen?"

"Exactly what I said. Exactly what you were thinking. My life was a paradise of money and attention. Isn't that the life you would expect the pampered daughter of the Laurences to lead?" Taking the apron from her waist she tossed it aside. "Enjoy your dinner, Zachary. I seem to have lost my appetite."

"Christen?" He called after her, stopping her as she reached the doorway. "What's wrong?"

"Nothing," she said without turning. "It's late. Posing for Hunter is a tiring task. I need rest more than I need food.

When you finish, put the dishes in the sink. When you're ready, your room is down the hall, the last one on the left.''

"Where's your room?"

"Next door."

"Hunter's?"

"Across the hall from mine."

"Will he be back tonight?"

"No. Nor probably tomorrow either."

"Then we'll be alone in the house."

"We've been alone before."

Without turning to face him she continued wearily down the hall, the leather costume of the Indian woman absorbing the light, clinging to her like a shadow. At her room she paused, her head bowed.

Zachary left his chair. He stood, watching her, the light from the kitchen turning the gold in his hair to burnished bronze. "Will your door be locked, Christen?"

An imperceptible tensing of her body and a slight shake of her head were her only reactions to the bold question. "My door won't be locked."

"Why?"

"Do I need a lock, Zachary?"

The dull, mindless hunger that was his constant companion exploded into full, throbbing need. His body was suddenly in agony. He wanted to sweep her into his arms, carry her over the threshold of her room, and keep her there until the falling snow was only a memory. He wanted her so badly that denying himself took every ounce of his strength. The heat of his need rose like bile in his throat. Lord! He wanted her. But not like this, tired and suddenly dispirited. When he took her, purging himself of her, she would be wild and fierce, scratching and clawing in her own passion, meeting his need with hers. Then he would be free of her.

"You don't need locks." His voice was a hoarse echo down the long corridor. "Not tonight."

She looked at him, trying to read his face through the gloom of the ill-lighted hall, wondering at the begrudging tenderness she heard in him. She sensed his desire for her. It was there when he walked like a marauding Viking into Hunter's home. He wanted her now, it was in every tense line of his body. She wouldn't delude herself that it was anything more than male need. There was no finesse, none of the subtlety of a seduction, only the blatant male intent to possess. Then, unaware, he probed the wounds of her childhood and left her hurting. Confronted by the specter of suffering he did not understand, he had relented.

He still wanted her. That hadn't changed. And in her hurt she would be vulnerable. He knew it, but had chosen to let her walk away. "A new rule for our ruleless game, Zachary?" She questioned softly. "Honor among adversaries?"

"Maybe."

"Honor suits you. You wear it well."

"Not as well as you think."

"Then it becomes you even more."

"I'll try to remember that."

"Good night."

"Good night."

Her door swung open. The light from a bedside lamp engulfed her, accentuating the lost look on her face.

"Christen," Zachary called to her.

She looked up, startled. "Yes?"

"I'm sorry."

"Why should you be?"

Zachary shrugged. "Perhaps for Benjie. For unhappy memories. For everything."

"You have nothing to be sorry for, Zachary. My troubles began and ended long before I met you. The wounds have healed. The scar tissue is well formed. The real tragedy is Benjie, and that there's nothing any of us can do for him."

"It still hurts you to be so helpless, doesn't it?"

"Did you think that would change?"

"Sometimes it does. People change. Values are lost. Goals shift. Needs change."

"Have yours changed, Zachary?"

"I don't know." There was a flicker of uncertainty that once would have been totally alien in the arrogant bravado of the street fighter. For a moment his attention seemed to slip away from her. His gaze focused on some inner thought. He shrugged, shaking his head as if clearing it of the dregs of sleep. "It's late and I'm keeping you. Sleep well, Christen."

Before she could answer he turned away and strode through the kitchen, letting the door bang behind him as he stepped into the night.

As she readied herself for bed Christen kept hearing his voice, husky and filled with doubt. *I don't know. I don't know.* The words danced like an endless madrigal in her mind. Sinking down into the bed, her head pillowed by goose down, she meant to ponder the meaning of this startling doubt. But as her world was wrapped in the deep, soothing silence of falling snow, she drifted into a mercifully dreamless sleep.

Her sleep was so deep she did not hear the latch of her door turn, but never open. She did not hear the hiss of a silent curse, nor Zachary's footsteps as he continued to the room beyond. The blue room.

Six

Zachary woke to a world of shimmering silence. A white stillness so deep the smallest intrusion echoed through it with the imperative clarity of a beckoning cry. The secret scrape of a footstep; the scent of coffee in the air; the bell-note of crystal—the sounds of morning drew him from the fitful sleep of a restless night.

He waited, still as the land beyond, as silent. His body quickening, anticipating each sound.

She moved beyond these walls. The woman he had loved. *Christen*. As strong as the land from which she had sprung. As spirited as the primitive creature in tattered buckskin. As elusive. As unforgettable. A woman he had never known.

Rising to a half-reclining position, his weight supported by one elbow, his attention turned to his immediate surroundings. The room was spartan, a creation of clean, masculine lines and subtle elegance. Its furnishings were handcrafted, on the blue-washed walls hung handwoven mats.

A bit of trivia learned, who knew where, then forgotten, clicked into place. The predominant design—the half diamond pattern in natural dyes—was Cherokee. A part of Hunter's heritage, appropriately adorning Hunter's home.

And there, in a small niche in the wall, Hunter's work. Framed by the richness of natural walnut sat a small figurine cast in lightly whitewashed terra cotta. The kneeling Indian maiden, slender and bare breasted, her arms raised to the sun in worship, was Christen. Her tawny body as perfect as he remembered.

"Ahh!" His low, explosive groan shattered the stillness that engulfed him. His pleasure in the graceful work was suddenly marred by an emotion so violent and ugly it drove him from his bed. With his chest heaving he walked, naked and trembling, to a window overlooking a valley blanketed with untarnished white. There was serenity beyond these walls but none within.

The reverent grace of the small figure was lost to him. He wanted only to throttle the man who knew her body so well he could reproduce it in such exquisite detail. His blood curdled thinking of the number of times Hunter's black eyes had touched her face, her breasts.

"How many times? How many?" The sharp rap of his fisted hand against the window reverberated through the room like a shot, the pane frigid beneath the sudden heat of his flesh. Startled by the sound, the chill, shocked by his outburst, Zachary raised his hands before his face, staring warily at the splayed fingers as if they belonged to someone else.

"Good God!" The words were hoarse, bewildered. This was madness and he knew it. Hunter was no lecherous savage, nor was he Christen's lover. He was a friend, a man

whose honor was his word and his art. It was only jealousy
that could find ugliness in the sensual figure of the sculpture. *His* jealousy.

Turning away from the window, he smashed a palm with
his fist. The lash of his anger turned inward, seething at
himself for letting the eruption of a possessive rage distort
and destroy his purpose. He had no claim on Christen, and
wanted none. He wanted only to be free of her, to rid himself of the memories that haunted him. He had not planned
coming to Laurenceville, but when the offer fell into his lap
he hadn't resisted. Providence? Fate? An opportunity to
exorcise the ghost of love.

Zachary turned to the coppery replica of the body he had
possessed. His lips quirked in a bitter smile, remembering
her as she had been. Slender, intense, beautiful. They had
been friends, antagonists, with differing concepts of medicine and the future. They were an unlikely combination. He
from the squalor and poverty of the streets, marked by the
blood of the battlefield. She sheltered and six years younger, years that might have been eons. She descending from
the subdued, but very real aristocracy of the founding family of small, rural Laurenceville. With all their differences,
the spark had been there the first day of residency, forming
a relationship that was challenging, competitive, and when
needed, supportive.

Supportive and more. Once, Zachary remembered with
mirthless smile, so very much more.

He had volunteered for special duty on the day that led to
the destruction of their friendship. It was a grueling job, a
long and frustrating deathbed vigil filled with heroic pro-
cedures of little success. Near the end of his second consec-
utive shift Christen slipped into the room. To offer respite
from his duties, to lend support. She came though they had
argued heatedly for days. He championing the virtues of

society practice, and full recognition of her talents; she for rural practice, its rewards, and contentment. It was an old argument, an impasse without solution. Yet when he needed her, she was by his side.

The patient was hardly more than a child, his once strong, healthy, sixteen-year-old body wasted and drawn by a simple virus turned killer. His prognosis was poor and growing poorer. Of the staff, only Zachary refused to admit defeat, and Christen understood. Together they worked for, prayed for, waited for a miracle. Then, in the lightless hell of the hour past midnight, their miracle happened. The unconscious man-child touched some unexplored depths of will and strength and began the uphill climb to life.

Weary but exuberant, Zachary had drawn Christen to him in celebration. Their first kiss was short and startling. Drawing apart in shock they stared, laughed self-consciously, stared again as if seeing each other for the first time. Then, with a soft sigh of homecoming, Christen stepped back into his waiting arms.

Zachary did not remember the next few minutes at the boy's bedside, neither relinquishing his duties to the attending physician nor the walk back to his quarters. But he remembered that they went arm in arm, Christen and he, neither letting the other beyond the touch of seeking fingers. He remembered that in the darkness of his bedroom her unclothed body gleamed with the lambent luster of the statue before him. He remembered the velvet softness of a tawny nipple, turgid and proud beneath his suckling caress. He remembered passion and gentleness. He remembered love unlike any a renegade from the brutal streets could know.

"I should have realized you wouldn't stay. We were too different," he said now. With the pad of his thumb he stroked down the line of the the terra cotta throat. "I should have walked away from what we shared as easily as you. I didn't. I couldn't. But I will.

"The winter is mine. There will be long, lonely nights, and I can be a patient man."

The house sighed faintly, rustling again with the subtle stirring of life. Like provocative incense, the aroma of coffee drifted to him, its fragrance rich, powerful and eloquent in a pristine world. Turning from the figure he gathered his clothes from their orderly heap. He was suddenly eager to see the real Christen, not Hunter's creation, however beautiful. But first a shower to complete the calming begun by the rap of his fist against the window.

His hair was still damp, beginning to curl back into the unruly wave that only careful brushing could control, when he left his room. Beads of water left by his cursory toweling stained the dark blue of his shirt to indigo. The shower that sluiced away the restlessness of the night had done nothing to soothe the hunger for Christen that had been building, slowly, inexorably within him.

He found her in the solarium, standing before windows that reached from floor to ceiling, looking out over a rugged gorge and the towering mountains that ranged beyond it. Dressed in a crimson shirt that hid her body, but left bare a handsome length of shapely leg, she leaned against a massive column. Her tousled hair, gleaming with diamond facets of moisture, cascaded over her shoulders. She sipped from a cup of heavy crystal, the dark brew a vivid contrast to the pale hands that held it.

How many times had he seen her like this? Rushing to her duties on the hospital floor, straight from her shower, her face scrubbed clean and innocent, her hair not yet tamed by the brutal control of a clasp. The white of her uniform heightening the color of a face that needed no artifice to be beautiful. How many times had he stood, his breath caught in his throat, waiting for that first glimpse of her? And each time she had been more beautiful than the last. But never as beautiful as now.

Beyond Christen, in the alabaster serenity that escaped him, a small deer appeared at the forest's edge. A mahogany shadow against the blanketed earth, his twitching nose sniffing the air. Cautiously he walked on spindly legs into the clearing. With his hooves lifting high above the white powder, in a prancing step he raced the length of the lawn tentatively, obviously unfamiliar with the snow. Half dancing, half galloping, he circled the clearing. Round and round he dashed, strutting, snuffling, a young clown, delighted with himself and with his discovery. Then, as if aware of his audience, he kicked up his heels and tossed his head, and trotted through the trees, disappearing again into the forest.

Laughing softly at his antics, Christen leaned her head back, her dreamy gaze fixed on a distant point. With the sole of one bare foot resting against the column, the shirt falling about her thighs, she was a figure in repose, turned by the glare of day to a familiar silhouette in ebony.

"Winter Morning," Zachary said in a low, thoughtful voice.

Christen turned, slowly, languidly. Silently facing him as if it were the most natural thing in the world that they should share the morning solitude. As if between them there was no need for the prescribed formalities.

"Just now, with the light behind you, you looked exactly as you did in *Winter Morning*." His solemn gaze slid over her with none of the anger the small terra cotta figure had incited. "I've wondered how Slade could capture that look of sheer joy. Now I know. He had only to look at you."

Turning from him, Christen pushed away from the column. Crossing to a serving cart that held a carafe, she poured a cup of coffee for Zachary and refilled her own. Returning to him, the pad of her bare feet was a silent whisper over a floor left bare but for a few wonderfully beautiful hand-loomed mats.

"*Morning* is part of a private collection." He heard the huskiness of sleep, deep in her voice as he took the cup she offered. "It's not been shown since the day it was bought."

"I know." Sipping from the steaming cup, watching her over its rim, he discovered her eyes were even greener when she wore red.

She waited expectantly for him to elaborate. When there was no more her brows drew down thoughtfully. "How did you discover Hunter's work?" Mindful of his taunts of snobbery she added, "Forgive me, but . . ."

"It's a little surprising?" He finished for her.

Christen shook her head, but did not speak.

"More surprising than that the favorite model of one of the foremost American Indian sculptors bears not one drop of Indian blood?"

"Touché," She tapped her forehead in a subtle salute, smiling for the first time.

Zachary watched the warmth of it spread over her face, over classical features that crossed any barriers of race or culture.

"You didn't answer my question," Christen prodded softly.

"How did I discover Hunter's work? Simple. A friend invited me to a fund-raising for the local museum in Brighton. Hunter's work was on loan particularly for the event. *Seasons,*" Zachary called the single name applied to each of four small, perfectly executed figures of Christen. "*Meditation.*" Again of Christen. "And *Grieving.*" Christen, of course. "It was later that I discovered *Winter Morning* and my favorite, the first of that series of works, *Awakened Enchantress*.''

Zachary was careful to let none of the excitement he felt with his first experience of Hunter's work and his startled recognition of Christen as the model, slip into his explanation. Nor would he tell her of the changes he had seen in her, changes interpreted and chronicled by Hunter. At first he hadn't realized the story the sculptures told, for he hadn't seen them in order. But as his first interest grew, turning into fascination, as the pieces were assigned their rightful order in his mind, he knew he was seeing more than the random works of a gifted artist. He was witnessing the growth of a woman.

First was the young enchantress, and Christen as Zachary had seen her in the fleeting interlude they shared. Then a time of grieving and meditation, then the healing of time and its seasons. And finally, the confident, joyous woman of the morning.

"This friend," Christen was puzzled by the quiet that had befallen him. "Is he or she the collector you spoke of?"

"Hardly." Zachary laughed, drawing his thoughts from their secret path, turning them to a madcap friend. "Marlee collects a number of things, but though she appreciates his work greatly, nothing by Hunter." He chuckled again, adding, "And little else that would be considered art."

"Oh?" Christen questioned.

"Charities, committees, publicity. Money. These are Marlee's collectibles."

"A true socialite."

"After a fashion."

"Are men among her collectibles?"

"From time to time."

"I see." Christen spun away, breaking the hold of the riveting gaze that captured hers at every turn. Throughout the whole unsatisfying conversation she had been keenly aware that his disheveled hair lay like silvered gold against his scalp, making her fingers ache with the need to tangle in its depths, drawing his lightly bearded face to hers. Once, in the joyous celebration of life that prerogative had been given her. One heedlessly discarded when love succumbed to fear and flight. Marlee, the collector of men, would not be so foolish.

"*Do* you see?" Zachary took a step closer, aware that the set of her shoulders was suddenly tense.

"No." Christen shook her head. "I don't, but perhaps I just don't understand."

"What don't you understand?" He was so close now that he could see the shallow rise and fall of her breasts beneath the soft cotton of her shirt.

"It's hard to accept you as part of a collection. The Zachary I knew wouldn't be." Again that slight disbelieving shake of her head. "He couldn't be."

"Do you hate the idea so much?" he said softly, watching her profile, the palpable throb of her pulse in her throat.

"I…" Her words seemed to catch painfully in her throat. The fringe of her lashes drifted down as if drawn by their own weight. "Yes," she murmured. "Yes! I hate it! My Zachary was wild. Free. Too much the rogue for a tame society. Too proud to become like one of my mother's lap dogs. Too honorable."

Zachary felt the beat of his own heart lurch out of control. His barely suppressed gasp caught behind a bitten lip. He meant to tease her but the backlash, a strange mix of possession and pride and bitterness, was far beyond his understanding. She had spoken thoughtlessly, unguarded, and with the mention of her mother, tangling her young, solitary past with the time they had shared. It made no sense.

Or did it? Setting aside his cup, he touched her shoulders, feeling the tension there in his own fingertips. For the first time he let himself wonder if there was more in Christen's life than he knew. Something about her mother, that reached beyond the past. Was it this that had driven her from him? It would be useless to ask Nathan, or Bell, or Hunter. None would violate her trust. The answer must come from Christen. But now there were things he wanted more than answers.

Sliding his hands down her arms and back again to her shoulders, he laughed softly, and was pleased at its natural sound. When she flinched at his touch and would have drawn away he held her fast. "Don't. If you knew Marlee, you would laugh too."

"Would I?"

"Umm hmm." He touched his cheek to her hair. It smelled of heather. "Marlee hates dogs. Little dogs, lap dogs, big dogs, any dogs. A color-blind Bohemian artist, or your wild, untutored rogue might be a different story." He deliberately used her possessive description of himself, goading her gently, hoping to draw her from the sudden blackness of her mood.

"Untutored?" Christen seized on the strange description, wondering what young woman would ever consider Zachary that.

"Honey." He took the cup from her hand and set it aside with his own. He turned her to him, chuckling now in earnest. His hand beneath her chin kept her from turning her face away. "Marlee is seventy-three. She's tiny, and frail, but with a will of iron and opinions to match. Her husband lived only long enough to lose everything and leave her impoverished. She doesn't collect art because she can't afford it. So she works, tirelessly and often beyond her strength. The money she collects are funds, to see that others like herself can at least enjoy the great artists through the museums.

"She was my patient for a short while, and in lieu of paying her bill, she decided I had some rough edges that needed smoothing. Even in her poverty, she is still the grande dame of Brighton. So how could I refuse? Who better to bully and insist and teach me?"

Christen remembered the stylish cut of the jacket he'd worn to Nathan's party. Without letting herself admit it, she'd wondered if Zachary, who had had little knowledge of clothing, had developed such impeccable taste on his own, or if a woman had lent a hand in the handsome choice. She raised her eyes to his, not aware that the shadow that had begun to darken them had lifted. "Marlee has done her job well."

"Sometimes I wonder. The rough edge crops up occasionally."

"As I'm sure Marlee intends it should. A woman finds a touch of the rogue attractive." She looked away, finding his direct stare too compelling.

"And you, Christen?" He had moved so close the heat from his body seemed to enfold her. "Do you find the rogue—" he paused, his hesitation putting a double-edged meaning on her word "—attractive?"

Christen touched her lips with a dry tongue. With her head still turned from him she watched snow sift in a fine mist from a drooping pine, wondering if its drifting coolness could soothe the burning weight of his hand from her shoulders. "I . . ."

"No!" One hand lifted to her face, curving about the arc of her throat, his thumb and forefinger resting against pulse points beneath the lobes of her ears. Exerting the gentlest pressure he turned her face to his. "Look at me," he murmured. "I want to see your answer."

A lock of her hair drifted over her face, catching in her lashes. A poor shield for the trembling awareness that must be evident in her eyes, but a shield nevertheless. "I've always found you attractive," she said, the soft words nearly lost in the crackling of the fire at the distant side of the room. "We were friends."

"Don't hide behind that, Christen. We were more than friends." The caressing stroke of his thumb halted. "Far more."

"Yes."

"Yes, what, Christen?" He had again that still sense of waiting. "What are you saying?"

"I'm saying we were more than friends." She brushed the veil of hair from her face almost defiantly. "I'm saying..." The harsh words dwindled into nothing, her own intensity paling before his. There was a whiteness beneath the dark of his skin, a grimness in the hard line of his mouth, the set of his shoulders. Christen stared transfixed into a face that offered no quarter. Compelled by a look that would accept no less than the truth, in a muted rush she blurted, "I'm saying you were the most attractive man I had ever known. The *only* man, Zachary."

They were not speaking of appearance, of handsomeness or beauty, and Zachary knew that neither would pretend that they did. "And now?" When she would have answered, his fingers against her lips stopped her. There was more he wanted to know. "Your door was not locked last night."

Christen shook her head.

"If I hadn't given you my promise?"

Again she shook her head. When Zachary took his hand from her mouth she repeated softly, "My door wouldn't have been locked."

A stifled groan crept though the room. Zachary heard his cry and knew it was the sound of one who had just felt his world falter beneath his feet. Hands that were barely steady rose, his fingers combing through her hair, smoothing it from her face. "If I took you in my arms now?" He stopped and in his silence found himself lost in eyes as fathomless as an emerald lagoon.

"I wouldn't run from you, Zachary. Not now." Her chin was tilted, but there was no belligerence in her face, only courage. "Never again."

"Christen. Christen." He murmured her name for no reason. Only because it was beautiful. Because she was beautiful. "Oh God! Christen!" He gathered her into his arms, holding her tightly, fitting her body to his. His lips touched her temple, tracing the line of her cheek. When he buried his face in the satin curve of shoulder and neck, barely visible beneath the collar of her shirt, he found that she was trembling.

"Don't be afraid, Christen." His breath cooled the hot flesh he had touched. "Not of this. Not of me."

"I'm not afraid, Zachary."

Her voice seemed to come from a great distance, like a whisper carried on the wind. He knew then that she understood as he did that this moment was inevitable. Whether yesterday, or today, or tomorrow, or the day after that, it was meant to happen. He knew, too, without understanding how he knew, that had he broken his word and broached her door in the night, Christen would not have turned him away.

Sliding one arm about her back, the other at her thighs, he swung her into his arms. "Where?" he asked softly.

"Here," she said as softly. "By the fire." Her cheeks were flushed, her skin moist, her look a little dreamy, as if she needed only his touch to make her real, to end the waiting.

He strode the length of the room, his heels a hollow sound on the wooden floor. At the fire by a mat of Cherokee design and blanket soft, he set her carefully on her feet. With the back of his hand he stroked the curve of her cheek and down the line of her throat to the cleft of her breasts. His fingers lingered at the first button of her shirt, then moved away. Surprising himself, he stepped away, his eyes never leaving her face.

"Zachary?" Christen's puzzled eyes searched his face. Then she understood. She was being given a choice. But only of time and place, for Zachary would make love to her, someday, somewhere, she had known it since the moment he stepped out of the shadows of the terrace and into her heart. Slowly, with fingers that would not quite obey, she began to open her shirt. She wore nothing beneath it, she had simply slipped into it as was her custom after her morning shower. Each button opened with an agonizing slowness. Each baring another small part of her keening body. At the last she hesitated, feeling that constant, unwavering gaze on her.

Christen did not fool herself that this meant to Zachary what it did to her. Beyond his veiled expression, and the heated quickening of his body, there was a coolness so deeply buried she had almost missed it. But it was there.

She loved him. That had never changed. He only wanted her. She lifted her head, turning from her concentrated effort from the silly, stubborn buttons. Zachary hadn't moved, but there was tension in every muscle, every sinew and the hot, glittering touch of his eyes was a caress. Yes, he only wanted her, but he wanted her badly, and for now it was enough.

Her shirt slid down her body, and gathered in a pool about her feet. Beyond the crackling of the small, vivid fire, Zachary's gasp was the only sound she heard. She felt, rather than saw the slow, marauding look that possessed her, even before he touched her. For the first time Christen felt pride in her own womanliness. She was glad her full breasts were firm and tawny crested, her waist small, the line of her hips lean yet curved.

"You're beautiful," Zachary said in an unsteady voice.

"You make me beautiful, Zachary, when you look at me as you are now."

Zachary did not respond. Instead he took the single step that would bring him back to her. Their bodies were almost touching, his fully clothed, hers bare, waiting. Again Zachary's fingers traced the line of her throat, pausing at the pulse at the hollow of her throat, as if to assure himself that this was the real Christen, not one of Hunter's perfect images. "I used to think of this. I used to lie in bed, wondering." His hand slid to her neck, gathering a fistful of her hair. "Wondering," he muttered harshly.

The pressure of his clasp as he drew her to him was painful, but Christen could make no protest if she had meant to. Zachary's lips covered hers, firmly, completely, insistently, but strangely gentle, and at odds with his guttural tone when he lifted his head to speak. "I wondered if Greg, or Slade, was touching you like this. Did any man kiss you like this?"

He kissed her again, deeper, harder, drawing her strongly against him in his sudden anger. His hand slid to her hip, holding her nakedness to the rough-clad thrust of his body. "Did any man hold you like this?" He spoke against her lips, not taking them from hers, not giving her room to turn away.

"Please." She pushed against him, struggling for the breath he hadn't allowed.

As suddenly as he had taken her, plundering her mouth as surely as the rogue she had named him, he stepped away again, leaving her to sway on her feet without his support.

"Do you know how much I hated finding Hunter was a young man. I hoped the artist who knew your body as well as I was an old, ugly man. Instead I found the never-photographed, reclusive sculptor to be a virile man."

"Hunter has never been more than a friend," she said with a false calm, refusing to be drawn into the battle that Zachary waged with himself.

"No. But there was Greg, and how many others? In five years there must have been others."

Christen opened her mouth to speak, to deny, but saw that it would be futile.

"Every time I kissed a woman, or held her, I wondered if a man was kissing you, holding you. How many were there, Christen? How many?"

"Zachary, don't."

"Don't ask? Don't keep score?" He made a sound that masqueraded as laughter. "Don't worry, Christen. After today it won't matter." With one hand he grasped the knit fabric of his shirt and in a single, lightning quick motion nearly ripped it from his body and over his head. Tossing it carelessly aside, his attention moved to the snap at his waist. As quickly as his shirt was discarded, so too were his slacks. He wore nothing beneath them. There was nothing to hide the magnificence of his body and its response to Christen.

"After today," he said softly, each deliberate word a separate entity, "none of it will matter. None of them. You will have forgotten them." He gathered her hair in his hands bringing her roughly against him. The first touch of their bodies was like a sheet of molten flame, burning, searing, holding them. "After today..." he muttered as his lips covered hers "...after today I won't care."

His kiss was long and deep, and for all his smoldering bitterness it was as gentle as the rising tide of desire could allow. Christen whimpered in pleasure, not in pain, against his mouth when his hands cupped her breasts. His thumbs stroked and teased, until her nipples throbbed, aching for the sweet surcease of his suckling. But her ease was not to come so easily. Zachary's palms moved down the length of her body, caressing, lingering, teasing again and again, even as his mouth plundered hers, his tongue teased hers.

He was a man who knew a woman's body. Her body. The sensitive areas, the erotic responses, and he left not one unexplored. When Christen thought she could stand no more, that this fine madness could be no madder, he proved her wrong. Holding her still against him with one arm, the other slipped between them, his hand slid through the furnace heat of their touching, his fingers trailed slowly but undeterred over the flat plane of her stomach, tangled for a moment in downy curls before slipping in a caress to the hidden, pulsing secrets beyond.

His first touch electrified. Christen shivered, her breasts rising with the gasp she caught and held. Her chestnut mane flew wildly about her face. "No," she moaned softly even as her body responded. "Ah no, Zachary." His name was a muted cry as she buried her face in his shoulder, shaking, hurting, wanting, clinging to him now as much for support as in passion. "I can't."

Christen vaguely heard her own cry and wondered what the words meant. Can't do this? Can't stand anymore? Can't wait?

Clinging to him, sobbing, whimpering, her nails digging into his broad back, her answer came through the red haze that enveloped her. She couldn't wait. She wanted Zachary now, here before the fire, with an untouched world of white at their feet. She wanted Zachary's body to be hers, hers to be his. She wanted. Wanted. But still his sweet torture continued.

"Zachary, please," she heard a voice that sounded nothing like her own plead. "I can't, Zachary. I can't."

"I know, love," he crooned in a hushed singsong against her cheek. "I know. Just a moment, to protect you."

Christen felt the rough scrape of the Indian mat against her back, and the chill of separation, and then Zachary was with her. His lips gliding over her, probing the soft indenture of her naval, touching warm and moist against her stomach, her ribs, tugging at her breasts. Each touch, each kiss, the gentle suckling, wound the tightening coil closer and closer to that desperate point of no return. When she was certain Zachary meant to drive her to madness, or to kill her with his bittersweet caress, he was rising over her,

"Now, love," he murmured. "Now." The thrust of his body was strong, powerful, but again, not ungentle. Yet Christen arched against him, and could not restrain a small tremor of keening pain.

The pain was a shock. Christen was too inexperienced even at thirty-three to know that a single encounter and five years abstinence would leave her almost virginal. What Zachary hadn't expected he understood, instantly.

"I hurt you!" Bracing himself on his hands he looked down into her dewy face. "Heaven help me, Christen. I didn't know."

"Shhh." Her fingers at his lips stopped his words. "Shh," she said again, her hand moved to tangle in his hair, drawing his mouth down to hers. "It doesn't matter," she said fiercely against him. "It's over." Her voice was low, her breath was hot and fragrant against his cheek. When her tongue stroked the grim line of his lips, he sighed softly, accepting her own delicate brand. When her hips began to undulate, he moved with her, slowly, tenderly, letting her set the pace. When she cried out again, there was nothing of pain in the sound. When she clutched at him, drawing him closer to her, she was a woman, with a woman's needs.

Zachary could no longer be gentle, but gentleness was not what Christen wanted. Her passion matched his, it thundered through her, the heart-stopping rhythm building and building until that sweet wild agony of completion left them shuddering and spent.

In the aftermath, Zachary slipped an arm beneath her, and with the other curled the edge of the mat over them. Drawing her to him he whispered from the edge of sleep. "This is how a man of Hunter's people slept with his woman, isn't it? Curled together in the mat where they made love."

Christen did not answer, for he was already asleep, his dark face tranquil in the flickering light of the fire. In his slumber he shifted, and turned, muttering unintelligible gibberish, only her name and his sorrow for her hurt sounding so clearly.

His hand curved possessively about her breast and Christen wondered if her greater hurt was yet to come. Zachary was a confusing combination of anger and tenderness. Yet even in her uncertainty, she was happy, and more fulfilled than she ever thought she could be.

Drifting through time, she held him, reveling in his weight pressing her down, imagining what it would be like to be his woman, to sleep with him night after night.

An inexorable memory cast its somber pall over her happiness. Her heart contracted.

Zachary's promise.

After today she would not remember her phantom lovers.

Zachary's promise.

After today he would not care.

The world swam out of focus. Tears she would not shed glittered on her lashes. "But today is not done, Zachary," she murmured.

Tangling her fingers in his hair, she dreamed, but only of today. Holding him, wanting him, wishing she knew him as well as she loved him, she waited while he slept.

Seven

Good morning."

For a moment after Zachary spoke Christen did not respond. With her back to him, her hair a tumble of dark copper over her shoulders, she continued to tend the fire. Then, as a log found its niche in a shower of sparks, she turned to him. "Hello." Her voice was like the smile that curved her mouth, comfortable and natural. "Good morning." The smile turned to laughter as she added, "Again."

With his long body sprawled beneath the mat, his head propped on his fist, Zachary looked steadily at her. He knew that she remembered as well as he that there had been no greeting between them, no formal greeting. Assuming a studied nonchalance he traced the raised pattern where she had lain, filling his lungs with the scent of her, remembering the heat of her desire beneath his touch. His composure deserted him, his long fingers crumpled the mat in his effort to still his trembling need to touch her now.

"Was this good morning?" He asked in a voice he barely heard as his own.

"Was it not?" she countered in soft spoken candor.

Slowly he released his grasp, his fingers caressing river-cane as supple as cashmere. "Christen," he murmured as the silk-smooth fibers reminded him of the satin of her skin. "Sweet Christen. I like the way we say good morning."

Her gaze fell to the slow, rhythmic stroke of his hand. Her head moved in a nod that could mean anything. Zachary found himself waiting, wanting more. Dark dread began to seep into that waiting and wanting, only to vanish in a burst of light when after an eternity she nodded again, whispering, "So do I."

With a thudding heart, wondering how a simple word could be both sensual and serene, he watched her as she knelt by the fire. Her shirt, carelessly donned, served little for the cause of decorum. Beneath the shadowy dishabille her body glowed like ivory. Her breasts, their rose tips veiled but not hidden by the clinging fabric, lay like delicate globes against her slender midriff. The shirt, gathered to her hips, offered a tantalizing hint of the line of gently curving thigh. She was more than lovely, yet had no concept of it.

She was completely without the cringing, belated modesty that could tarnish a shining moment. There was in her a stillness that spoke of sweet secrets and contentment. With her palms resting on her thighs, her fingers laced and her head bowed, she was a replica of *Meditation*. He wondered now, as he had years ago when he'd first seen the handsome terra cotta figure, if the tranquility that lighted the lovely face touched her heart as well.

But this was Christen. A warm and exciting woman who gave herself without reserve and with a trusting innocence, not a figure preserved for all time in clay. That thought shuddered through him, the truth of this moment twisting in him like the keen, thin blade of a rapier. Denying what his body would believe, he searched the small figure, seeking the woman who had taken the trust he offered to no other, accepting it in the warm embrace of night as the gift of love it was, only to walk away in the cold, clear light of dawn.

Through some tear in this gentle, giving facade, he tried to unmask the woman who had dwelt since that night in the dark, frigid desert of his heart. He searched, but Christen was not the creature he had come, callously, to seduce. That woman did not exist. He knew now, as an ancient anger flickered and died, she had never existed.

"Christen." He murmured her name hoarsely, waiting for her head to lift, her eyes to meet his. At last, cool and level, from beneath the sweep of sooty lashes her gaze rose to him. He saw again her serenity. But there was something more in her face, in her expression and the glowing well of her eyes. Indefinable things, whose roots lay in a pain that was older than their friendship, older than his love, older than his obsession with her. Things he had been too blind to see.

He groaned so softly she could not hear. Disgust, ugly and violent, burned his cramping throat like bile. Bitterly he wondered where was his great triumph? Filled with self-loathing he looked away, for he couldn't bear to look at her, at the lovely body he had taken in vengeful lust, and would take again and again, because he could never have enough of her.

"What have I done?" The words burst from him unchecked. With a guttural snarl he rolled to his feet. The mat, caught in a brutal grasp, flung over one shoulder, offered no illusions about his virile body.

Drawn from her thoughts by his cry, Christen watched as he stalked to the window. His white-gold hair curled against a nape permanently tanned from stolen hours spent sailing the ragged coast of the Carolinas. The long, massive line of his bare body was wrapped haphazardly in the mat, and he was once more the sun-baked Viking who ravaged her heart and trampled pitiful promises. But she was no longer the child who promised never to love a man to the exclusion of all else. She was a child no more. In his arms, she had finally become a woman. "You haven't done anything I didn't want you to."

He flinched as if she had plunged a dagger into him, but did not move from the window.

A sound of sorrow caught in her throat. The natural male arrogance that once had frightened and infuriated, and intrigued her was gone. His distant gaze looked beyond the valley and the mountains to some private agony. Had it been like this when she fled her lusty young lover? Had she done this to him then? And now, somehow, again?

Rising to her feet she knew it must not be like this. Her Zachary was brash and bold; the firebrand who walked the waterfront poised, ready, confident; the raider of timid hearts who taught a woman what it meant to love.

I've learned the completeness of love, she thought. And the consequences are well worth the risks. She smiled softly to herself and knew that for the first time in many years the shadows that lurked in the depth of her heart would soon be gone. In the hour she had watched her lover sleep, she had walked alone through the chaos of her childhood. With brutal honesty she had sought out those memories, facing them with the grace and forgiveness of a woman. With that grace came understanding, and in understanding her mother, she had begun to understand herself.

At thirty-three she could recognize what a girl barely out of her teens could not—the need for a lonely woman to love and be loved. The need that became a desperate addiction in her mother. And yes, she admitted freely, a need Zachary brought to her own life.

Christen would never pretend that she could forget the hurt of her mother's abandonment. But forgiveness begot peace. The wounds that crippled her were healing. No fear chained her heart, for there was no place for fear in her love for Zachary. What he wanted she would give, for as long as he wanted her. And when he was gone, she would remember. It would be enough.

As she walked to him her footsteps were slow and unfaltering and nearly silent, but with each hushed tap of her bare foot on the polished wood floor, the muscles of his heavy shoulders rippled with the effort of control. Undercurrents of strain pulsed through him like a deep, hidden tide. Zachary, who had always been cool under fire, was like a high voltage wire. The wrong move, the wrong word and his precarious constraint would explode. She wondered if this was how he had been on the streets and in the jungle. Totally aware, his nerves raw, perceptive.

She stopped just short of him, her breath unwittingly held as she waited. Across the valley the sun had begun to play a game of hide-and-seek with a band of scudding clouds, turning the world below to a study in a gray velvet and glittering crystal. At another time she would have watched, fascinated, loving the spectacle, reading its portents. But now her whole world was Zachary, a world of fire and ice with a man of passion, who without warning had become a remote stranger.

"A penny," she said, forcing a light note into her voice. When the corded tendons of his neck grew tighter, she wanted to slide her hands about his waist, press her cheek to the hard, square back and hold him. Instead, because she knew he would find her touch anything but soothing, her fingers tangled into a double fist as she heard his short bark of laughter.

"I'd need change, they aren't worth even that."

"They are to me."

"You wouldn't like them."

"Try me." She touched him then. Her hand on his arm was cool, but the slight weight of it burned him.

"No."

"Look at me." She ignored the wooden resistance as she tugged at his arm. "You won't find answers in the snow."

When he turned, his gaze blazed with such violence that she instinctively looked away. Drawing a shuddering breath she stared down for a moment at her fingers curled over his forearm, then slowly, taking courage from the startling and beautiful contrast of her pale flesh meeting the darkness of his, she challenged his stare.

His features were as stark as granite, his lips a thin, unforgiving line. "You look so grim," she said. "Is what you're feeling so bad?"

"Bad enough," he replied gravely.

In that moment her strength nearly deserted her, then she remembered that this was Zachary, that she loved him, and must take the bad with the good. "Then perhaps you'd better tell me," she said quietly.

"You asked why I came to Laurenceville." His voice was hoarse as from lingering passion.

Christen nodded. "On the terrace at Nathan's. You said you came for Nathan's sake."

"Did you believe Nathan was my reason for coming?"

"I believed he was a part of it. But I think we both knew that was only a part of it."

"I respect Nathan. In a very short time he became a good friend. But given the opportunity I would have come here even if I'd hated him. Sooner or later I would have come anyway."

"For me."

He would not lie to the woman before him. "Since our last day together, since the night I made love to you—" he stopped abruptly wondering how he could put the truth into words without destroying her, without destroying himself.

"Don't try to sugarcoat it, Zachary. Say it as you feel it. Perhaps the truth will hurt, but I think not so much as lies already have." Bracing herself, she waited.

"Lies, Christen, or evasions of the truth?"

"Is the result not the same?"

"I suppose it has been."

"Then why don't you tell me why you came to Laurenceville?"

Zachary swung away, the mat cleaving across his body as he leaned against the heavy frame of a window. For a time he seemed to immerse himself again in the distant land.

"I don't think a day has gone by that I haven't thought of you." He shrugged slightly. "Not always an overt thought, but you were always there. In a drift of perfume. In a sound of laughter. You were every woman I saw, and none of them. When I kissed a woman I was kissing you. When I made love to a woman...." Softly he struck the dark wood at his side. "Even at sea there was no escape from you. Did you know that when the light is just right the sea is exactly the color of your eyes? You were everywhere I turned. I couldn't escape you."

"So you came to Laurenceville."

"Yes."

"To exorcise your ghosts."

"Yes."

"Have you hated me that much?"

"I haven't hated you. Dear heaven! If I had it would have ended with the hate. If I hated you I wouldn't be here now."

Christen wondered if hearts could really turn somersaults, or if, perhaps, they really could soar. Her own was doing a very good imitation of both. Zachary made no declarations of love, but he had admitted she was an indelible part of his life. As he was of hers. Hunter knew. Had Greg? she wondered. Had he waited patiently for the day she would put her mysterious lover out of her life? Had he hoped for the impossible?

So long as Zachary lived he would be her only love, but she'd been too young in experience to know that running from him could not change it. It was an older woman, wise from the lessons of her goodbyes, who now spoke softly to him. "Have you exorcised your ghosts? Can you leave and never think of me again?"

She stepped between Zachary and the window, her hands sliding beneath the mat to clasp his waist. Looking up into his stern visage she asked with a husky voice, "Have you had enough of me, Zachary?"

He gasped as she stroked his side. Her touch, her words enveloped him like a sheath of flames. He reached for her, his words a low rumble deep in his chest. "God help me, no. I can never have enough of you."

This time there were no buttons to deal with. The tiniest shrug of her shoulder sent the cotton shirt flowing like a fiery mist down the length of her body. Before the crimson garment reached the floor she felt herself enfolded by the only garment Zachary wore. Beneath the mat their bodies met, her breast rising to press harder against him as her arms lifted to bring his lips to hers. Zachary's body branded hers, as her mouth caressed his.

They had no need for words as they turned together to the fire. A blaze leaped and danced, fanned by the sweep of the mat being spread again before the hearth. Zachary heard it snap and spark like miniature firecrackers, then there was only the soft sound of their breathing. And when the world spun crazily out of orbit, there was Christen, holding him, whispering his name.

The fire had died to smoldering embers and the room lay in shadows when Hunter entered. With the silent step of his mother's people he moved to the sleeping couple. Crouching by Zachary he touched his shoulder lightly, saying, "Dr. Steele, Zachary."

Zachary woke instantly, his body stiffening before he realized that the face that hovered over his was Hunter's. He relaxed, but only a bit. He knew something would have to be wrong for the man to come to them now. "What is it, Slade?"

"You should wake her now," Hunter said in a hushed tone. "The weather is worsening. I should get you down the mountain as soon as possible. If this storm keeps developing, Christen will be needed. We all will."

Zachary nodded his understanding, careful not to disturb the woman who curled, lovely in sleep, at his side. He would do as Hunter said, but not yet. He wanted no one with them when he woke her. He wanted the waking after love to be his alone. A treasure to keep. It would be this he would take with him when he left her. This rather than the satiation of lust he had meant to have.

He looked into Hunter's face and saw that beneath the concern there was recognition. He respected Zachary's reluctance to share this awakening in the presence of another. Was it the unspoken covenant one warrior afforded another, Zachary wondered, or simply the arrogance of the possessive male? Whatever it was, Zachary knew Hunter would be no different with his own woman.

His woman! The words made Zachary's body quicken, not with passion, but with a sense of wonder that set his heart pounding and his blood singing in his veins. Christen was his woman? No! A thought as beautiful as this was impossible. They were too different. They had proven that years ago. She had been wise to leave him, before they had begun to tear at each other, destroying the only good thing left for them, their memories of a friendship.

There was no future for them, but he'd had this day. His hand curled gently about Christen's shoulder in his need to cling to an impossible dream for the little time left to them.

"Zachary?"

Hunter called his name as only Christen and Marlee did. Now there were two people other than Christen who called him Zachary. One his friend, the other Christen's. He wondered if the day would come when they would both desperately need these friends.

"We'll be ready to leave in half an hour," he promised, giving them more time than they needed, but time he coveted for himself.

"Sorry." Hunter shook his head, a look that approached pity on his face. "Fifteen."

"All right, fifteen." Zachary agreed and found he was speaking to empty air. Like a ghost Hunter had faded away, giving Zachary and Christen the last precious seconds alone. It was Hunter's tacit approval of what had happened here between them. Hunter's approval of Zachary himself, and Zachary was a little astonished at how important that approval was to him.

The brooding darkness of the day crowded in on him. The bright sunlight that had flashed in early morning like white fire over glittering snow, then played hide-and-seek among the drifts of reddening clouds, was lost beneath a seething bank of gray.

Hunter was right. The day looked dangerous and time was passing quickly. He had promised fifteen minutes. From the look of the sky Zachary feared Hunter had been too generous. Stroking a strand of chestnut hair from Christen's face, tucking it carefully behind her ear, he leaned to kiss her. Her lips were warm against his, alive and inviting.

"Hi," she whispered as he drew away.

"Not 'good morning?'" He teased, loving the sleepy look of her, the brightness that lighted her eyes like a million stars.

Christen stretched, her body rising to brush his, her arms lifting in a graceful arch and coming to rest at the back of his head. Lazily one hand trailed down his face, over his cheek, to trace with the utmost care the line of his lips. Slowly the smile on her lips faded, the sparkle in her eyes dimmed. Gravely she said, "I'll keep this morning with me forever."

"Yes." However eloquent he hoped to be, her honesty took his breath and tied his tongue. He could only mutter the single word and nod mutely.

"Have you wished you could stop the clock and the world as well? To keep a moment that you knew could never come again?" she said with dreams in her voice.

As she stroked his lips he saw that sadness tempered her serenity. He knew she recognized their differences as clearly as he. She understood as well that this had been a wonderful interlude, but it could be no more. But did it hurt to dream, he wondered? Could it hurt to admit those dreams?

"Yes," he said. "I've had my share of impossible dreams."

"And some you made come true." With each breath she drew her body brushed against his, her nipples were like delicate rosebuds against the tangle of golden down that covered his chest. The small medallion he wore, his angel, was warm from his body when it slid in a molten path over the slope of her breasts. Moving her hand from his face, she clasped the delicate figure in her palm. "This is your reminder of all you've escaped and the dreams you made come true."

"She's more than a symbol. She's been my guardian angel, seeing me through the worst and the best of my life. She reminds me that the impossible is sometimes only a little more difficult than we realized." His voice dropped to a rough, hurting tone, "But only some things."

"I know." Christen released the breath she had not realized she held, waiting for this answer. The heat their bodies shared suddenly seemed not to be enough, and for the first time she saw that the fire had died long ago, and the bright day was overcast. She shivered, but not from the chill of the room. To ward off the blackness that threatened she said, "Once I thought this day was impossible and yet it was ours." They were words of a hope she had not yet admitted.

"Ours alone," Zachary murmured as he leaned closer, touching the lips that seemed to wait for his, saying with the kiss the words he couldn't find. Long and deeply he kissed her, holding her to him. As he struggled to keep the moment, in his mind time ticked away, stealing her from him. At last, forcing himself to move away from her, he brushed a tear from her lashes saying softly, "Now it's over. Hunter says a blizzard is brewing. We have to get down the mountain. He gave us fifteen minutes. I'm afraid our time is almost up."

"Hunter was here?"

"You were asleep. Somehow he knew we needed this time together. He's a perceptive man."

"He's known me for a long time. I think he's seen more than I realized over the years."

"As an artist?"

"As a friend, and as a man with his own disappointment. He gave us the time he was denied." As if following a written script, a clock boomed the hour. The day was passing rapidly. It was late afternoon but as the room had grown increasingly dimmer, Zachary's features had fallen into heavy shadow. With the storm coming darkness would come early, and getting down the mountain would be difficult enough.

"Hunter has a sixth sense about the mountains and the weather." She looked away from Zachary to the gloom of a lowering sky. "If he said fifteen, then fifteen it must be."

"He said you would be needed."

"We all will."

"He said that, too. Shall we go?" He moved from the folds of the mat and rose. In an easy motion he slipped into his slacks. As he returned to her, looking down at her, seeing again all the beautiful things she was, he wanted to forget the storm, that Hunter waited, and take her into his arms. Instead he offered his hand. "Come with me, Christen."

She did not speak as she took his hand. She was not ashamed of her nakedness, yet she was grateful for the shirt he draped over her shoulders, his shirt with his scent filling her lungs.

They walked the corridor together. At her room he left her, leaving only his kiss to warm her. In a trance she gathered the few garments and personal items she would need, then folding her hands she sat, waiting for Zachary.

His tap on her door was not long in coming. At its sound she gathered up her bag and joined him.

"Ready?" he asked.

With a start she realized that he had no luggage. He had only the clothes he wore now. Of course, he hadn't come prepared to stay. The time he had given her alone was meant to give her space, a time to find an even keel before she had to return to the real world. "Yes," she smiled up at him. "I'm ready."

At the door as they donned heavy parkas and knitted caps, Christen explained the temperature was dropping rapidly and would continue to drop as the cloud cover thickened over the sun. Though he listened and believed, Zachary was unprepared for the shock of the cold. His first breath felt as if it froze his lungs.

The vehicle Hunter called the Cat was idling in the drive, its exhaust turning to frozen vapor almost instantly. Zachary saw that it was small, and the enclosed cab was obviously meant to accommodate two average-size people at the most—and neither he nor Hunter were that. With the two of them squeezed into the cab there would be no seat for Christen. Hunter would be occupied with the Cat. Negotiating these treacherous curves in icy snow and in near darkness would be a task that required his unencumbered attention. But had it not, there was still little doubt in Zachary's mind that he would be the one to hold Christen through their journey.

Hunter took Christen's bag and stood it in the back. From his pocket he produced a pair of gloves for Zachary. "You have your gloves, Christen?" he asked.

"In my pocket."

"Good. The cab is heated, but should we have any sort of difficulty we'll be glad for warm hands." He looked at Christen and grinned. "Sorry, honey, but you just lost your seat on the bus. You have the misfortune of having to suffer being stuffed in the Cat with two overgrown brutes. I don't think you want either of us to sit on you so why don't you let Zachary get in and then you climb on his lap. Since the Cat offers minimal amenities and heat, you'll probably be more comfortable that way."

"Fine," Christen answered.

"Zachary?" The flash of white teeth in Hunter's dark face showed that he knew Zachary had already made the decision ahead of him.

In answer, Zachary mounted the steps and seated himself in one of the two separate seats in the cab. When Christen grasped his wrist and stepped on the track of the Cat, he swung her into the cab, into the circle of his arms and settled her on his lap. "Comfortable?"

"Yes, but will I bother you? Will I be too heavy?"

His chuckle was a low, musical sound. "Will you be too heavy for me? The answer is no. Will you bother me? The answer to that one is yes. Damn straight, sweetheart, you'll bother me."

Christen turned, their gazes met, and simultaneously both burst into laughter at the intended connotation of his reply. Their laughter served to put them at ease, determining the path they would follow in the aftermath of intimacy. Christen knew the undercurrents would always be there. One unthinking word or gesture and they would be pulled into the undertow. But with caution they could be friends as they had years ago.

As she settled back against him and the hard circle of his arms embraced her, she felt Zachary had read her thoughts and understood. She heard the deep rumble of his laughter begin. As her own laughter rang out, she was sure of it.

"Can anyone join in?" Hunter asked as he took his seat behind the steering wheel and engaged the gear, "Or is this a private joke?"

"Sorry, Hunter," Zachary said. "But this one's private."

"Yeah." Hunter shifted the gears again as the machine began to gain speed. He flashed them his brilliant grin. "Somehow I thought it would be."

For awhile the two men talked, learning about and from each other. Christen dozed off, still listening.

"Is this sort of storm common here?" Zachary asked.

"We have our share of snow, but not usually of the magnitude this storm promises," Hunter answered.

"How could you be caught so off guard?"

"These mountains can do unpredictable things to weather. It's the same with the sea. You sail, I understand."

"Christen told you?"

"No, actually, I heard it from my mother, who heard it from Nathan, who heard it from his doctor friend in Brighton."

Zachary laughed. "Talk about grapevines."

"Almost as good as an Indian tom-tom."

"If there is such a thing." Without waiting for a reply to his comment Zachary continued. "Your mother is an unusual woman."

"You get no argument from me on that."

"Has she actually lived with her tribe on the reservation?"

"Until she was eighteen and left with my father."

"You were born on the reservation?"

"No, I was born in England, and lived for a number of years among my father's people."

"From your tone, I take it the experience was not a happy one."

"Let's just say my mother wasn't the bride they would have chosen for their only son, and I certainly wasn't the heir they wanted for... Never mind, my father's dead and mother brought me home, making everyone happy."

"What Hunter isn't telling you is that he's heir to an earldom with its castles and lands," Christen intervened for the first time in their conversation. "If he wanted them."

"Which I don't, and won't." There was no bitterness in Hunter's voice. "My father loved my mother. It wasn't a prerequisite that his family love her, too. Or me."

"How did you come to settle in Laurenceville?"

"Nathan and my father were friends. When he died, mother notified Nathan. Nathan was a widower who had just inherited his orphaned grandson."

"Greg?"

"Right, Greg." Hunter nodded. "She needed a job, he needed a housekeeper. So I grew up here in Laurenceville a few hours drive from the reservation. Close enough for mother to spend time with her people."

"You lived in Nathan's home along with Greg and Christen?"

"No, until I went away for awhile, she kept her own home."

"But you knew both well."

"Greg was a fine boy and and even finer man, if that's what you're asking. He championed my cause and Christen's as well. I think he was very probably responsible for making us the people we are. He kept us both from going off the track at a time when we could have grown bitter and rebellious. I was a half-breed, and as in any place where two races live closely, there was prejudice. Not a lot, but enough to hurt."

"And I was the poor little rich girl whose mother no longer wanted her." The cabin was dark now and Christen found she could speak in the anonymity it afforded. With Hunter at her side and Zachary's arms about her she found the courage to speak of things long hidden. "She was the most beautiful woman I've ever seen. Far more beautiful than I could ever be. But all she could see was that I was younger. I was in the first bloom of womanhood and she saw me as a threat. My father had been dead for three years and she was a very lonely woman. She had lovers. I wasn't competition, but she thought I was."

"So when she didn't want you around anymore, Greg took you to Nathan, and Nathan took you in and became your legal guardian," Zachary finished for her.

"Exactly."

Zachary folded her even closer to him, his cheek rested on the knit cap that covered her hair. "If Greg were here today, I would give him my thanks."

"We all would," Hunter said in a note that ended the discussion. The snow that had melted during the day was turning to sheets of ice. The sharp, looping switchbacks were growing more dangerous with each passing turn. He needed no distractions.

Sensing the increasing danger, Zachary grew tense and watchful. Straining his eyes to seek out the farthermost perimeter of the headlights, he watched for any unexpected elements—a fallen tree, a rock slide, a cave-in in the road. His body was taut, his eyes burning, but Christen filled his mind.

How many times, he wondered, had he taunted her, called her a little rich girl? In the beginning he had been teasing, but it still must have hurt. Only weeks ago he had flung the name at her, cruelly. Not once had she defended herself or refuted his accusation.

He had called her sheltered and privileged when nothing was farther from the truth. Perhaps she hadn't fought in the streets or in a steamy jungle, but her life had been filled with its own ugliness. She had known losses greater than his. Only his grandmother and Jacobi had really mattered. Christen had lost first her father, and in a fashion her mother, then Greg, and now she faced the threat of losing Nathan. She faced it all without a whimper.

There was nothing he could do about past losses, but there was one that was tearing her apart, one he could help with. Benjie. He could take over his treatment and bear the brunt when the child's losing battle ended, as it soon would. He could do this for her before he left.

Christen leaned heavily against him. He knew by the weight of her that she slept. Folding her collar more closely about her neck he said in a low voice that she would never hear, "You're one tough lady, sweetheart. You could give lessons in strength to far rougher and bigger people."

"She's only as tough as she has to be," Hunter said in a voice as low. "Don't give her cause to prove it." He grimaced then and shrugged. "Sorry, didn't mean to eavesdrop. Good ears. A gift of my ancestors."

"It doesn't matter," Zachary replied. "And I won't hurt her if I can help it."

"Your word on it?"

"My word."

"Can't ask any more than that."

The first lights of the village loomed ahead. The clack of the Cat's track over a narrow wooden bridge woke Christen. They rode in silence until Hunter guided the machine into the drive in front of Nathan's home. The lights blazed throughout the house like a beacon for weary travelers.

"Bell's expecting us," Christen said.

"Probably with a pot of her special hot chocolate waiting on the stove. She always had that for me when it snowed. With peanut butter cookies fresh from the oven. You see, there are some advantages to being half-breed. You get a mother like mine."

"How would she know we were coming down?" Zachary asked, then with a heavenward lift of his eyes he drawled, "I know. I know."

In unison the two men chanted, "A gift of her ancestors."

When their laughter died, Christen asked. "Is this a private joke, or can anyone join in?"

"Sorry kid," Hunter began.

"This one's private," Zachary finished.

"I sort of thought so," Christen said.

With a sense of camaraderie they walked arm in arm to the door. When the men stepped aside for her to precede them, she lagged back and muttered something about cleaning her boots. The door banged behind them before she stepped to the edge of the stairs. She looked out over the mountains that were now only dark hulking shadows. Up there somewhere a light burned, the light in Hunter's solarium.

There were lights dotted over the mountainside, but she knew that none was the light she sought. That light burned far away at the crest of the mountain, and in her heart.

As she stood with her face lifted to the sky, the first snowflakes of the new storm began to fall. Before she turned to the bright lights and laughter that filled the house, her hat and parka were dotted with white.

Eight

—

I'll expect you all for dinner by eight," Bell said as she set a platter of scrambled eggs and bacon in the center of the kitchen table.

Hunter, who had not returned to his mountaintop in the month since the snowstorm asked with a suspiciously expressionless face, "On this lovely Monday morning is that an invitation, a suggestion, or a command, Mother?"

"Considering that the hours you've all been working have been too rigorous, it's all three," she retorted sternly. "In reverse order."

"Yes ma'am." Hunter's grin broke through as he ducked his head.

"And you?" Bell addressed Zachary.

"Who me?" He looked at her in wide-eyed innocence. He never ceased to enjoy the jousting between the mother and her bear of a son.

"Indeed."

"Well ma'am, seeing as how I do like your cooking, I'll do my best."

"I'd like more than your best. I'd like for you to *do* it, and see to it this young lady does, too."

"Me?" Christen echoed, looking up from her plate absently, aware that she hadn't heard the preceding conversations.

"Do you know another young lady who's been skipping meals because she's working far too hard? Who wades through snowdrifts, fords swollen rivers, and drives over mountain roads meant only for goats in galoshes?"

Christen smiled briefly at the analogy, then, remembering the epidemic of influenza that had swept through the extended community in the days following the snowstorm, she sobered. "What was done was necessary."

"I won't deny that and you can't deny it's taxed your strength. It would tax a gorilla's strength, and you're not a gorilla. You've lost weight. You're too thin. I shudder wondering what would happen if you should catch the flu, too."

"But I haven't and I won't. This hasn't been a solitary effort. Zachary was with me. And Hunter's left his own work to gather dust while he's helped out. They've worked as many hours and traveled as many miles."

"Undoubtedly. And you make my point. Big as they are, a lost pound or two won't hurt either of them. You didn't have it to spare in the first place."

Christen bowed before the logic of loving concern. "The worst is over. We were lucky the first cases appeared only days before the snow. Thank God it imposed a natural quarantine, keeping down the spread of infection."

"Making it necessary for you to practice medicine from the back of a truck," Bell added drolly, refusing to let her make light of the grueling hours spent taking medical care over the mountains and through the valleys to scattered and isolated homes.

"The worst is over," Christen repeated. "I'm reopening the clinic full-time today."

"Alone?" Bell asked sharply.

"Gin will be there, Bell." She touched the capable hand that rested on her shoulder. "Thank you for caring, but I'll be okay, and soon we'll all get some rest. Then I'll work at gaining back the weight. In fact," she straightened her spine. "If someone will pass me the bacon, I'll start right now. I'm ravenous."

"Save a slice for me," Hunter said around a mouthful of toast.

"Dibs on the one that's burned on the end," Zachary interjected a teasing note back into the conversation. "That's the way I like it. Burned."

"My bacon is not burned, Dr. Steele," Bell drawled to the sound of tinkling silver as she tapped her foot.

"It isn't?"

"No." A small smile quirked her mouth even as she tried to suppress it. "It's extra crispy."

"I stand corrected. Pass the one that's extra crispy. That's the way I like it."

"Just so long as you like it."

"That I do, ma'am. Without a doubt."

"Then prove it by getting home for dinner, and see to it that Christen does, too."

"You set me up for that one, didn't you, dear lady?" Zachary chuckled and cast a conspiratorial look at Christen.

Christen smiled back, trying to catch the spirit of their fun, hoping no one realized how miserably she failed. Looking about her she saw a room as comfortable and warm as the woman who ruled it. A place of shelter from trouble. A haven that invited one to breathe deeply the richness of spice and baking bread and bask in the warmth of sunlight sparkling through spotless windows. There were fresh flowers scrounged from heaven knew where in the midst of winter, a feast for the weary eye.

Bell's kitchen, the heart of this home, was a place of laughter and love. Christen felt like a traitor not to be cheered by it.

The profound sense of loneliness that engulfed her in its icy prison made no sense. As she watched the camaraderie of her breakfast companions she felt small and selfish. It was rare that Hunter accepted anyone into his small circle of chosen friends. He trusted only Bell and Nathan and herself. And Greg. Now he was drawing Zachary into that select group, and Zachary, once the eternal loner, joined willingly.

She should be happy, she thought as guilt became an unbearable weight. Happy that Hunter and Zachary, each reluctant to form close relationships, and each for his own reasons, were becoming such splendid friends.

Friends. Her friends. Zachary and Hunter.

Watching as Zachary joined in teasing Bell, Christen smiled suddenly and ruefully, as much at herself as at him. Perhaps that was her talent in life—turning a lover into a friend.

Was that her malady? Had she developed a gigantic case of blues because Zachary worked through the crisis of the snowstorm and the epidemic tirelessly, cheerfully. Sometimes ruffling her hair playfully. Sometimes chiding her when they both worked to the dropping point, but never once recalling the morning he had taken her in his arms, teaching her again the joys of a woman.

He had been so careful not to complicate their lives, to exert no pressure. He had been gallantry itself, and rather than being grateful, she sat in Bell's wonderful kitchen, watching him with a drooping lip and jealous eyes.

Dammit! Did she really have it, what ever *it* was, that bad?

Yes!

Her glass slipped from her fingers, spattering cranberry juice over her wrist, turning her white cuff a pale shade of rose.

"Christen!" Laughter faded abruptly from Zachary's voice. "Have you cut yourself?" She heard the taut edge of concern as he took her hand in his, turning her palm, checking her fingers, assuring himself she was unharmed.

"No!" The denial burst from her. "I'm fine." Jerking her hand from his and grasping a napkin, she muttered something inane and senseless about early morning clumsiness as she dabbed at the spill. It didn't matter what she said, nor even that she was unharmed. What mattered was that she could not bear his touch. Not like this, Not here, not now.

"Christen?" He said softly. Only her name, asking a question she dared not answer.

Drawing her blind stare from the spreading stain, her eyes met his, holding, keeping, seeking her own answers, finding none. For an agonizing instant she almost hated the pleasant face he wore. She was glad when after a long critical look he turned from her, blocking his tender concern from her sight.

She did not need his gentleness, nor his concern. She needed the flame that would melt any ice, the wild, forbidden sweet that soothed the bitter. She needed the bold, passionate Viking who cared nothing for gentleness and friendship. She needed Zachary, who stepped out of the shadows with challenge and lust in his eyes, and played a ruleless game.

Suddenly bewildered by the intensity of her reaction, Christen found herself watching him. Mystified and enchanted she studied him, furtively, through lowered lashes. He'd brought a sense of beauty and desperateness to her life then moved calmly beyond reach. As she longed to love him whatever the cost, he became a maddening paradigm of honor. Now, comfortably at home in Bell's kitchen, he sprawled gracefully over a chair, dressed in jeans so faded and soft they clung to his thighs with a loving faith. She saw him smile. She heard him laugh, the quiet sound wrapping itself about her like an embrace. He moved, flexing tired shoulders, pulling taut the open collar of his shirt.

He leaned nearer, the clean, masculine scent of him filing her lungs. With sunlight catching in his hair, the flash of his smiling eyes touched her, lingering warmly on her, including her in his world. And the mystery and the paradigm were forgotten.

He was again the man, warm and alive, who had shivered when her questing fingers tangled in the swirling pelt of his chest; who suckled at her breast and caressed her; whose body joined with hers, losing himself in the consummate power of ungovernable passion. He was Zachary, and in the quicksilver moment when he had been truly hers, he called her love.

Memories. Yesterday's realities, the substance of dreams. Her dreams.

High atop a world wrapped in a gossamer mantle of white, their hearts and bodies had merged, and for one blissful day their differences were forgotten. In an enchanted world that knew neither time, nor place, they were simply man and woman, and there was love. But bliss is elusive, and theirs was a world, not of crystal palaces, but of life and sometimes death. Yet paths destined for a collision course had righted themselves. In the aftermath she had looked for love. Zachary had settled for friendship. Perhaps it was a greater wisdom that understood that lovers might be friends, but friends must never be lovers.

She had promised herself she would be what he wished, for as long as he wished. But, she wondered bleakly, how did she stop herself from never wanting more, needing more. Never was a long, long time.

"Never, Christen?" There was no laughter in Zachary's voice. Worry creased his brow as he watched her carefully.

"What?"

"You said, 'never'. As if you were disturbed, or angry."

She hadn't realized she'd spoken. Shaking her head to clear it she said, "It's nothing. I was just thinking out loud." She was suddenly aware that all attention was focused on her. Bell stopped in the act of taking a pan of cinnamon rolls from the oven. Hunter paused in refilling his cup. In suspended animation they waited for an explanation.

"I was thinking about a problem at the clinic," she managed at last, wondering wildly what they would think of the true direction of her thoughts, of the ache only Zachary could fill. As only he had. She couldn't bear any more. She could not sit in Bell's kitchen remembering.

As her gaze fell on the stain that crept over the table, she realized it had been only moments since she had dropped her glass. Thoughts that seemed to move through her mind ponderously had been fleeting. It had taken no longer than a heartbeat to discover what a fool she was.

"I need to change," she said almost shrilly as she held up the spattered sleeve. "I'm afraid I've ruined your tablecloth and the napkin, Bell."

"A little juice won't hurt them. It won't even hurt your blouse if we get it into soak pronto." After one appraising look, searching Christen's harried face, the housekeeper took the napkin from her, muttering with a bantering gruffness, "I'm glad you're a better healer than you are a maid."

"So am I." Christen tried a laugh.

The housekeeper clucked and raised an eyebrow at the sodden food on Christen's plate. "Since our areas of expertise are firmly assigned, why don't I get you another plate?"

"Don't! Please. I couldn't eat another bite."

"Child, child," Bell began, then relented. "All right. I'll let you off this time. But I do expect you home for dinner. Promptly and with good appetite." She swooped down to press her flushed cheek against Christen's paler one. "Run along and see to that blouse. Put it in the tub with cold water. I'll collect it later and launder it."

Christen seized on the excuse to escape the confinement of the kitchen. She rose hurriedly, sending her chair reeling. Only Zachary's quick catch kept it from falling against the wall. As he righted it his troubled gaze followed her from the room.

Neither man moved or spoke. Bell was the first to stir, moving from the table to a counter. The swaying of her silver bell was a small sound in the cavernous silence. Its music had faded when she spoke. "I've never seen her so on edge."

"She's working too hard," Hunter declared. "When a patient can't get to her, she thinks she has to go to the patient—unless one of us beats her to it. The roads've been nearly impassable for anything but the Cat and four-wheel drive vehicles for weeks. First because of the snow. Then the mud and flooding that followed this burst of warm weather was as difficult."

"You prefer the arctic to false summer?" Zachary asked, his mind was on Christen, barely registering Hunter's observation or his own question.

"Let's just say I prefer frozen ruts to the quagmire."

"I see your point."

"I'd rather slip and slide over these hills, than to dig myself out of them. Speaking of digging out, in case I have to, we'd better get started. I've a list of medications that should be delivered before evening." The list was in Hunter's head. Zachary had never seen him write anything down. "If I don't get it done," Hunter continued, "Christen will be out doing it this evening. A road that's tough in daylight can be a real bitch in the dark and she has no business hauling that big truck over them."

"But we both know she can," Zachary said as Bell turned to listen to them.

"I said shouldn't, not couldn't," Hunter parried. "You know as well as I that anyone as tired as Christen is more likely to have an accident."

"Then it's up to us to see she doesn't, isn't it?"

"In one fashion or another."

Zachary's gaze met Hunter's, finding in it none of the threat delivered so succinctly a month ago on a mountaintop. There was warmth, now, in those dark eyes. In some inexplicable way, Hunter knew the man who had come to Laurenceville bore little resemblance to the man who had later wakened with Christen in his arms. Zachary's voice was rough when he murmured, "I'll see that she doesn't get hurt."

"As well as you can," Hunter qualified for him. "Not even you can give guarantees."

"As well as I can," Zachary repeated. "I wonder just how good that will be."

The insistent warble of the hall telephone interrupted. Hunter waved a hand, forestalling Bell. "I'll get that."

The Indian woman nodded as her son left the room. Setting aside a plate filled with cinnamon rolls she moved to Zachary's side. "She is not as you remembered."

"What?" Zachary's mind turned from his thoughts with a jolt. Then, with a slow shake of his head he said, "No. She isn't what I expected."

"How could she be? When you first knew her, even then, even in her twenties, she was still a girl of little experience. A brave one who ventured out into the world, yet held herself aloof from it. Still, she attracted friends, as someone as lovely as she would. But keeping them always at arm's length. One friend, a special one, did not heed her finely drawn boundaries.

"Christen Laurence was unready for such a man as Zachary Steele. In her poor experience she couldn't know that few women would be. When courage failed her she did the only thing she knew to do. She fled.

"Now Zachary Steele has come to Laurenceville with vengeance in his heart. And behold! He finds the girl who has lived in his heart for years isn't the woman he thought her."

Lulled by her soft voice, the perfect diction, the unique phrasing, it was a moment before Zachary understood the full import of Bell's observation. His surprise was short-lived, because it seemed natural that she would know and understand. "Have you known from the first?"

A shake of Bell's head stopped him. "I knew little at first. Because I knew Christen, I knew what would frighten her and drive her back to the sanctuary of her beloved mountains. It was only after Nathan brought you here, when I saw how she looked at you, how you looked at her, that I knew the rest."

"Are you psychic? How could you see so clearly? One look and you know what's in my heart. You know of the years Christen's been a part of me."

"It does not take a psychic to understand. You're here. If what was begun between you five years ago had ended, you would not be."

Zachary found in the dark eyes of the mother the same compassion as the son. He saw his own image mirrored in their darkness. The image of a man who came to exorcise the memory of a girl and discovered a woman.

"It's true, is it not, Zachary? You would not be here if it had ended?" Bell asked softly, insistently.

"No." His admission was a guttural sound, rumbling harshly from his throat. "I wouldn't be here if it was ended."

"At first there was anger in you and I feared you would hurt her. Since the mountain I know you will not, if that choice is within your power."

"You believe that!"

"Yes." She leaned over the table, the knuckles of one fisted hand tapped lightly over his heart. "Because you've changed here."

Bell put into eloquent words what Hunter said with a look. "Like mother, like son," Zachary growled roughly, but with no rancor.

"Yes," Bell agreed, unperturbed by his gruffness. "Hunter would know. He has few friends. Because he cares deeply about those few he is intuitive about them. Especially about Christen. They're more alike than you might think."

"I know some of Hunter's history. How his father's family treated both of you. The difficulty of his mixed heritage."

"There are other problems. Greater ones, but they molded the man as well. Because of them he has turned to his talent. And in his own hurt he learned to care for those about him who hurt. He had a sixth sense about it." She slipped into the chair beside Zachary, her hand rested over his. "He knows that something irrevocable happened on the mountain. More than the coming together of a man and a woman."

"He told you?"

"Only in confirming what I already knew. That it was more than a sexual encounter. It was a beginning."

Zachary's laugh was a mirthless sound. "He's wrong. It was an ending. Not one as I thought it would be, but an ending nonetheless. Our differences were never more real than they are now. Christen and I are further apart than we've ever been."

"Are you? You're here in Laurenceville. You're Christen's friend again. That's a beginning. Perhaps there will be more. Perhaps not."

"We're too different for more."

"You were, but are you now?" Bell's dark eyes bored into him as if they saw something he did not yet know. After a long, quiet moment she smiled. Releasing his hand she rose saying, "My son thinks not. He's wise beyond his years, his artist's eye sees more than most. Be patient with yourself and with Christen. Wait. See what the days ahead will bring."

"Riddles, Bell?"

"Unsolicited advice," she said with a chuckle.

Hunter's low, tuneless whistle reached them before his footsteps tapped over the quarry tile. "That was Lucy Foster." He gestured toward the telephone. "She called last night, I was fortunate enough to catch the call. She was watching reruns of Ben Casey."

Zachary groaned. "She's having the same symptoms. Whatever they were."

"Yeah. Thank God it wasn't prostate trouble." Hunter's grin was devilishly innocent. "I remembered the original episode, and the cure, and advised her what to do."

"She listened?" Zachary hadn't had the dubious pleasure of dealing with the tipsy Miss Foster, but Ginny had prepared him should the occasion arise.

"Only after I convinced her I was a great medicine man."

"You used that particular terminology, did you?" Bell asked.

"Sure. She thought it meant I was a great doctor. When it turned out I gave her the right cure, she was convinced. So much so, she called today to thank me."

"I'm surprised she remembered," Bell said.

Zachary's interest was captured by another of Hunter's comments. "How could you remember a particular episode? You had to be a kid when you saw it."

"I remember everything I see or hear. I have to," Hunter explained cryptically. "It's a habit that served me well this time, wouldn't you say?"

"Undoubtedly," Zachary agreed. A strong suspicion about his handsome friend was beginning to take shape. Random observations and occasional comments were beginning to make sense. When he was sure of the direction of his suspicions, he would discuss them with Christen.

"Ready, Zachary? Christen left for the clinic while I was on the phone with Miss Foster. Won't do for her to get too big a start on us."

"Not if we intend to see to it that she doesn't overwork so badly today."

"Look, Christen's right, the worst of the epidemic is over. If yesterday is any indication, today should be a light day. The roads are so much better most of the patients can get to the clinic under their own steam. And there can't be that many prescriptions to deliver. Tell me your delivery list and I'll cover it. That way you can go in to help Christen."

"Tell you my list?"

"Right. I'll drop you off at the clinic and take it from there."

"Sounds good."

Zachary pushed back his chair, murmured his thanks and dropped a kiss on Bell's cheek as Hunter had, and followed the larger man from the room.

"Hurrah! It's Friday. And thank God this week saw the last case of the flu." Ginny draped herself inelegantly over a chair, a grim look on her face. "Blast it all, there's nothing I hate more than snow."

Christen burst into laughter. "Gin, you say that every year."

"And every year I mean it."

"Until the next snow and you make a beeline to buy wax for sled runners."

"Well, I do hate it when it's all brown and yucky."

"That's mud, Gin, the snow's been gone for some time."

"One comes after the other as surely as thunder after lightning and a cigarette after good sex. Or," she held up a qualifying hand, "like a cigarette used to come after good sex."

"Quit again?" Christen drawled.

"The cigarettes, yes. The sex, no. When the powers that be tell me that's bad for my health, I'll, well, that's where I draw the line. There's nothing like it, sugar." Ginny grinned, her classic face lighting in her delight in needling her boss. "You should try it sometime."

Christen casually tossed the chart of her last patient for the day on the desk before the older woman. "Maybe I will."

"Ohh?" Ginny's sculptured brows rose a notch.

"Someday."

"Rats. I thought maybe you meant with the good doctor Steele."

"Nope! Remember the skier I promised and all the little hotdoggers we were going to make to populate the slopes?"

"I think he was the hotdogger and you were going to populate the slopes with skiers."

"Same thing. Anyway, I've found him. He was in before lunch with a sprained back."

"The one with the long black pigtail and the pearl in his left ear?"

"The very same. He proposed."

"Before or after you gave him something to ease his pain?"

"After. Does that mean he'll be fickle?"

"You can bet on it. Won't give you the time of day until the next time he falls down a ski slope."

"If you have trouble with your fickle skier, I'll be glad to oblige."

"Zachary!" Christen whirled about to face him. "I didn't know you were there."

"I know."

"We were just kidding around." Christen felt the heat of embarrassment rise in her cheeks. In the past week neither had exactly avoided the other, but their conversations had been short and few, now he had heard this nonsense. Oh well, maybe better this than the silence. She shrugged and smiled at him.

Zachary returned her smile, his gaze holding hers just a fraction too long. For an instant she thought she saw the smoldering of hidden passion in his cool blue eyes. When his look strayed lightly over her flushed face and his smile became a grin she knew her imagination created that passion.

Without rhyme or reason a question triggered by Ginny's learned observations popped into her mind. Before she could stop it, she heard herself asking, "Do you smoke, Zachary?"

"Do I what?" He seemed first bemused, then amused. Chuckling deeply he said, "I have in the past, as a kid before I knew better, and again in Nam. On a rare occasion, under undue stress, the habit crops up again. But for the most part, I don't smoke." A rakish brow lifted as he looked at Ginny. "Not even after good sex."

"Murder," Ginny slid another notch lower. "You heard."

"All of it."

Ginny abandoned any attempt to reclaim her dignity and dissolved into a hiccupping laugh. "Do you disagree with anything?"

"Not a word."

"I think it's time to change the subject." Ginny sobered. "How is Benjie?"

"Better, I think. His cold's almost gone, but his mother wanted to be certain. To make sure he didn't come in contact with any stubborn flu bugs I had her wait until the clinic was closed to bring him in." He looked at Christen. "I'd like for you to look at a test I left in the lab. I need your opinion. When you've seen it, come in and say hello. I think you'll like what you see. He's gained a pound or two and his color's better." In spite of the good news Zachary shook his head regretfully. "Now, if he would only smile."

Overwhelmed by the sadness on his face, Christen laid a consoling hand on his shoulder. It was the first time she had touched him deliberately in weeks. "I'll check the test and be in directly."

"Thanks." Covering her hand with his own, he squeezed it gently and walked away.

"He took over Benjie's care to spare me the heartache," Christen murmured. "And look at him."

"He takes it pretty hard, doesn't he," Ginny said behind her.

Christen compared the compassionate man she saw with the hard, unfeeling man who had first arrived in Laurenceville. Somewhere in the days and nights as they worked side by side that calloused man had ceased to exist. Christen's face glowed, a secret smile curled her lips. "Ginny," her smile turned to laughter. "The real Zack is back."

"Where's he been?"

"I have no idea. I only know he's back."

"Well I think we're all suffering from battle fatigue. It's the only answer for today's nonsense. Thank goodness Brighton college has decided the weather's improved enough to resume their monthly volunteer services, starting tonight. So, while they grub around getting mud on their pretty little lab coats, you have a whole weekend to rest and recuperate. When you get home don't forget to switch off the phone. The whiz kids will catch any calls here at the clinic and you needn't worry. I tease about them, but this is a group of super kids. Brighton Medical College is about to let loose a flock of good doctors." She picked up her keys, frowning down at them. "Was there anything else? Anything I need to do?"

"I can't think of anything. If something crops up, Zachary and I can handle it."

"Would you like a little advice?"

"I would not."

"I couldn't make even one suggestion?"

"Not even one."

"I should go home, huh?"

"Definitely. Good night, Gin."

"'night."

Benjie's report looked as good as Zachary hoped. Reading the values, comparing the new with the old, Christen's heart soared. No one more than she understood Zachary's need for a second opinion. When one ached and hoped and prayed for a change, even the tiniest improvement could be viewed as a miracle. Conversely, to keep from overreacting one tended to take a pessimistic view, resulting in a complete loss of objectivity. But today, Zachary needn't doubt himself. "A good report," she murmured, folding the lab sheet and tucking it into his chart. Good, but, she reminded herself, for Benjie it was a relative term. "If it buys a little time maybe..."

Christen spun her seat around, thinking as she did how precious time was to the tiny boy. Every second he lived was a second closer to the discovery of a treatment that would work for him. "There will be one," Christen's voice broke. "There has to be."

Rising, she laid the report aside. There was a reverence in the act, as if it were a precious document. In those numbers and values, there was hope. Walking briskly down the corridor, eager to give Zachary the news, Christen felt happier than she had for days. Even the fatigue that was her constant companion of late seemed to lessen. Outside the examining room door she paused, then, deciding it was foolish to knock, opened it and stepped in.

The room was in near darkness with only the failing light of day to illuminate it. In the shadows, in a chair that barely contained his bulk Zachary sat, his body relaxed, his lashes heavy on his cheeks in sleep. And Benjie, who had done no more than endure her touch, slept as well. He lay cradled in Zachary's massive arms, his baby curls a silver gleam against the scarlet of Zachary's shirt. One tiny fist was tucked beneath Benjie's chin, the other clasped a chain, the golden angel lay hidden within his tiny hand.

Christen watched them with a sense of wonder. They were beautiful. Man and child, a portrait of trust. No matter what the future held she would remember the ruffian who held a fragile child with incredible tenderness and found a lost compassion.

With brimming eyes she brushed a lock of hair from Zachary's forehead. When he stirred beneath her touch, she murmured softly, "Shh, sleep, my weary love, sleep."

Long after he subsided and the steady rise and fall of his breathing resumed, she watched him. This was the man she had given her heart to and her body. The man she loved.

Leaning to him she kissed his temple, lingering, feeling the beat of his life's blood beneath her lips, the warmth of his flesh against hers. This moment she would keep in her heart.

Soundlessly she left them, stepping into the corridor, shielding her eyes from the harsh glare of its light. Deep in thought she made her way to her office to wait for Benjie's mother to return from whatever errand had called her away.

Nine

———

"I'll be leaving tonight after dinner," Hunter said.

Christen nodded, but did not speak.

"Will you be all right?"

"Of course I will, but I'll miss you," she said, linking her arm through Hunter's. Fallen leaves crackled beneath their feet as they strolled through Nathan's dormant garden. "It worries me that you've sacrificed six weeks of your time."

"It wasn't a sacrifice, Chris. Working with you is a pleasure."

"My dear friend, I thank you for that." Christen rested her cheek against his arm, sliding her hand into his. "But we both know it's past time for you to retreat to your lair and begin your work. You've lost time to make up."

"Wasn't lost. I got to watch my favorite model in action. Sort of a study of anatomy in motion."

Christen burst into laughter. "What anatomy? The one covered with heavy coats and boots and mud?"

"The very same." Hunter tugged her to a halt. She stood patiently while dark eyes searched her face. "You will be all right. I see it. You've been different these last few days. More at peace with yourself and Zachary."

"I think I am. I've finally accepted something you've known for a long time. Some things are meant to be, some are not, and there's nothing we can do to change them. We live, we learn, and we grow. Within that premise we change what we can, and make peace with the rest."

"It's a lesson with a price."

"For both of us."

"We'll both survive. A bit battered, with little pieces of our hearts torn away, but each time a little wiser."

"A little." Christen looked away from those all-seeing eyes, keeping from him the pain that was still too raw to be completely hidden.

Hunter's big hand cupped her cheek, his fingers smoothed her hair. As softly as the breeze that rustled the leaves about their feet he said, "You love him."

"Yes."

"You aren't going to tell him, are you?"

Christen shook her head, then murmured, "No."

"Don't you think he has a right to know?"

"I don't think it would matter."

"Good God! Chris, are you blind? Can't you see?"

"That he loves me? Yes, I think he does in a way. But there's more than that. We've always wanted such different things in life, and in the long run they've been more important than what we might feel for each other."

"You don't know that."

"Yes I do." Sliding her arm back through his she began to walk with him again. "There's an element now that makes it even truer. Zachary came to Laurenceville for a lot of reasons. I was one, but one he didn't understand himself was his dissatisfaction with his life, that he'd lost sight of his goals. That's changed. He knows again who he is and what he is, and even better, he's the compassionate man I knew. He'd lost his way, now he's found it."

"Through Benjie."

"They've learned from each other. When Zachary's time here is finished he'll leave behind a legacy of trust and take with him compassion. The single element that will make him more than the brilliant diagnostician he's always been. He's in touch again, with his patients and with himself. I can't complicate his life now. He deserves the chance to go back unencumbered to his old life and achieve the success he worked so hard to gain."

"If he asked you to go with him?"

Christen stopped, head down she stood with her eyes closed. Her hand fumbled blindly for his as she turned to him. Her lashes lifted slowly, her green eyes shimmering. "God help me, Hunter," she whispered hoarsely. "I would go anywhere with him if he asked me."

"Ahh, Christen." Hunter gathered her into his arms. "It hurts. I know how it hurts." Folding her close to him he rocked her gently, stroking the russet fall of her hair. "You've waited so long to give your heart, while every man who's ever met you has been more than a little in love with you. Now the man who's caught the golden ring will walk away and never know. Sweetheart, I'm sorry."

Like a lost child Christen clung to him, her body trembling in silent anguish. A chilly wind nibbled at her cheeks and tousled her flowing hair, but could find no fault in the protecting shelter of Hunter's embrace. In time her shudders subsided. She stood quietly, bathed in the light of the setting sun, warmed by the arms of her childhood friend. He offered strength and comfort, but Christen knew that no one understood better than Hunter that only time could ease the hurt of loss. Sighing softly she stepped away. Her eyes were heavy-lidded but dry. Scrubbing at her cheeks she managed a wry smile. "I promised myself I wouldn't do that."

"You won't, not with Zachary." He stroked her face. "Would it help if I stayed?"

"No, but thanks. I guess that was just something I needed to get out of my system. There won't be any more tears."

"You're one strong lady."

"Not as strong as I'd like to be."

"Strong enough. There's nothing wrong with tears, or with needing people. So, if you need someone to lean on, just for a little while, remember my lair is only a mountain-top away."

"I'll remember." Rising on tiptoe she drew his face to hers, and holding it in her palms, she smiled at him and kissed him lightly. "There's a woman out there somewhere in tomorrow who doesn't know yet how lucky she is. But the day she finds you, she'll know. She'll love you, Hunter, and know how wonderful it is to be loved in return by you."

"What would this wonderful woman want with a dumb half-breed?"

"Don't, Hunter. Don't do this to yourself."

"It's all true, you know."

"She won't care what blood runs through your veins, or what you can or cannot do." She touched the strong line of his jaw, looking into a face that held the pain of countless hurts. "Nothing will matter except love."

"You're an incurable romantic, Dr. Laurence." Hunter caught her hand in his. Lifting her fingers to his lips he said, "Now, if you're ready, I think we'd better go inside. Mother and Zachary will be waiting. You know how important this night is to her. First night, she calls it. The beginning of a new year."

"The day she likes most to have those she cares for about her." Christen smiled, feeling as though something was settled. As if speaking aloud her thoughts made them easier to accept. "It's been the same since I was fifteen, when I first came to live with Nathan. She'll miss him this year."

"She'll have Zachary to fuss over instead."

"For a while." When her green gaze met Hunter's there was courage and resignation in her smile.

Hunter threw an arm about her. "Let's go in to dinner."

Hours later, when the candlelight dinner was only a memory and Hunter long departed, Christen wandered the silent house. Sleepless and alone, she pondered the quiet Christmas that had come and gone. In the library her aimless meandering halted. Here the holiday still lived. Tiny, multicolored lights on the tree still burned, spangling the walls like a kaleidoscope. The pleasant scent of evergreen drifted through the room like a spring breeze. Christmas and the promise of spring, the two were forever united in her mind by that scent. Drawing a deep breath she savored it for the last time. Tomorrow, on the second day of the new year, as part of Bell's holiday ritual, the tree would be gone.

It was New Year's Day, the traditional time to take stock of the past and look to the future. Zachary had been with her three months. He would be here three months more. That, Christen thought, is my past and my future, beyond that I will only exist.

She looked at the tree, its branches drooping with finery. Christmas, then spring. And Zachary would be gone.

As if daring her to forget time's passage the clock in the hall struck the hour. One o'clock. In the profound quiet that returned Christen sighed. It was tomorrow. Gathering her nightclothes tightly about her she turned to go, certain she would not sleep, but knowing she must try.

From the corner of her eye she caught sight of an ornament hanging precariously from a limb of the tree. Reflexively she reached to right it, setting the gold bangle that encircled her wrist afire with the gleam of a thousand lights. The bracelet was classic elegance. The inscription that lay against her flesh read simply, Merry Christmas from Zachary.

A gift. As impersonal as her own to him. A key chain bearing the image of an angel. A seasonal sentiment that would soon be tossed aside and forgotten.

Her hand froze, her mind stopped in mid-thought. Neither breath nor whisper nor footfall ruffled the stillness. She waited in a silence that grew deeper. No sound or move betrayed him, yet she knew. Zachary was there, beyond the light, watching her.

A subtle awareness charged the air. Her heart lurched into a hammering pace that set her head spinning. His eyes were on her, she could feel them touching her, touching her body silhouetted by lights that turned her demure cotton gown to a veil of translucent gossamer. A blush turned her skin feverish, but she made no move to gather her nightclothes about her. She would not hide.

Her hand fell away from the fragile ornament. The restlessness that had driven her from her bed became a familiar hunger. Her need for Zachary trembled inside her, waiting.

"Beautiful." The word was a low, guttural rasp.

With her fists clenched, her nails scoring her palms, Christen replied, "All Bell's Christmas trees are beautiful."

"I didn't mean the tree and you know it."

Lashes that had lain like shadows against her cheeks fluttered open. The shuddering breath she had drawn became a soft sigh. Slowly she turned to him, her emerald eyes finding his. "Yes, I know."

With slow, silent steps he moved nearer. So near she could feel the heat of his taut body, the power of the hot, marauding gaze that consumed her. She yearned to step into his arms, to feel the rippled velvet of his corduroy shirt teasing her breasts and the slide of his rough jeans against her thighs. She hungered for the essence of him, that bold masculinity that taught her of womanhood. She wanted, but dared not take, for something in his manner stopped her. His own need was as real, she could sense it. God! She could feel it. Yet, there was something different about him, a controlled violence she did not understand, a somberness that tempered even the candescent torch of lust.

"Christen." His voice was troubled, a rough grating whisper. His eyes narrowed. No part of her escaped the piercing intent of his crystalline regard. She was held fast by it, like a butterfly beneath the collector's spike. After an eternal moment he looked away. With the same intensity he turned on her, he explored the room.

His darkening gaze absorbed its muted elegance, touching in turn each treasure. He nodded once, a gesture of bleak resignation. There was serenity here. It was here she belonged.

"I was wrong." His voice was again in a guttural rasp. In it the same reluctance. Words wrenched from a well of disquiet as he abandoned his silent perusal.

"Wrong?" A frown creased the smooth plane of her forehead.

"I tried to force you into the life I wanted for you. I told myself it was because I recognized your talent. I fooled myself into thinking it was because I wanted what was best for you. Because I was older and wiser, remember?"

"You did." Christen protested. "You were."

He kept her from saying more with an angry gesture. "It was all a lie. Yes! You were the best. And yes, I wanted you to use those skills, but the real truth is that I wanted you for myself." There was fury in him now, tamped, seething, barely restrained. "I was so desperate to keep you, I took you to my bed, never bothering to consider if it was right or wrong for you. I only thought that I could hold you that way, if no other.

"When I woke and found your note I knew I'd made a terrible mistake. I'd driven you away. To keep from hating myself, I tried to hate you. I spent years working at it."

Christen remembered the hard, cold man who confronted her on a deserted terrace those months ago. It was easy to believe he hated her. "You succeeded in your effort."

"No." With a gentle hand he brushed back her hair, his fingers lingering in its silken strands. "The first time I saw you again I knew I couldn't hate you. You were magnificent there in the darkness, with moonlight in your hair, and all I could think of was how it would be to make love to you."

Christen felt suddenly giddy. She needed to speak, to ask so many things, but her mouth was dry, her throat paralyzed. Shaking her head in disbelief she croaked, "But you were so angry."

"With myself, for wanting you. I tried to deny my feelings. For years I tried."

"You were angry the night you followed me to Hunter's."

"Angry and jealous and scared," he admitted in a rusty growl. As her face froze in shock his lips curled in a grim parody of a smile. "I was wild with jealously and scared of what I'd find, and madder than hell that it mattered. When I saw how wrong I was, I should've turned around and run down the mountain."

"But you didn't."

"No. That was my first mistake."

"The second was making love with me?" Her question was half hope, half dread.

He looked down into her expressionless face, seeing the cool brittle control. "Yes, Christen, it was a mistake."

"I see." The giddiness turned to a dull throb. What more was there to say? With a shrug of her shoulders and gathering the strength left her, she turned to go.

He grasped her shoulder almost roughly. "Don't turn away. Dammit, Christen," his fingers dug into her flesh. "Look at me."

Numbly she did as he commanded. She was frozen inside, no pain could touch her now. "All right." Her gaze was steady, filled with frigid calm. "I'm looking."

He withdrew his hands, his fingertips tingling from the force of his grasp. One hand fell to his side, the other strayed absently to the pocket of his shirt.

"You have no cigarettes, Zachary."

"Old habit." His smile was a grimace.

"Is that what I am?"

"No! Dammit, Christen, you're the only good thing that's ever happened in my life. And for once I'm trying to do the right thing." His hands reached again to touch her, then curled into fists as he stopped himself. "God in heaven!" he whispered. "Don't you know it's almost more than I can do to keep from ripping that gown from you and taking you here on the floor, before the tree or Bell, or anyone else who might choose to come along?"

She stared at him, a look of wonder on her face, her eyes the green fire of a distant star. "I . . ."

"Hush. And don't look at me like that or I'll break every promise I've spent the evening making to myself. The little sanity you've left me tells me another broken promise would be another mistake. Haven't I made enough mistakes where you're concerned?"

His hands were still fists, his teeth were clenched. The angel visible at his throat rose and fell in trembling violence. "You aren't cut out for an affair, and that's all we could ever have. I've just learned that. You knew it years ago.

"I've been angry with myself for so long, I suppose I'd almost forgotten I was angry with you, too. For being right, for knowing that you belong here." His voice dropped a note. "You've been happy here?"

The abrupt change, the unexpected tenderness threw her off balance. For a moment she wanted to lie, but his honesty forbade it. "I've been happy, for the most part."

"Happier than you could have been in Brighton."

She felt the glittering force of his gaze, searching hers. She wanted to explain, but in her heart she knew it was too late for explanations. In the end she only nodded saying, "Yes."

"This is your home. I can see that now." He drew a shaky breath. "Do you remember how we argued about it?"

"I accused you of being an opinionated male chauvinist."

"I called you a stubborn, provincial fool, when all the time you were the wise one."

"Not as wise as you think."

"No explanations, no excuses." He touched her lips lightly, tracing their contour, pausing at the corner, remembering that it dimpled when she smiled. "Let's just agree that we met at the wrong time, in the wrong place, in a world that was mine, but could never be yours."

"I didn't mean to hurt you," Christen whispered against his fingers.

"A part of me has always known that. I can't say the same."

"You didn't come to hurt me."

"I thought I did. I tried."

"Each hurt was followed by a kindness."

"A vicious cycle. I came tonight to end it." Realizing that his hands had strayed from her face to her shoulders, he drew back as though her touch scorched him. "In three months Nathan will be back. We have that much time to rebuild what we had before I decided to play God with your life." His smile was real now. "Can we?"

Christen looked at him. He was tired. The tension between them, the epidemic, and the battle he fought for Benjie had exacted its price. He was tired, but he was in touch again, with his patients and himself. He deserved the chance to go back to his old life, unencumbered, to make it the success he worked so hard to make it. Her own words, uttered only hours ago, branded her mind. If agreeing would give him a measure of peace she couldn't deny him. "Yes," she said, offering her hand. "We can."

He took her hand, holding it, his thumb stroking the pulse at her wrist. "Hunter got a kiss in the garden. Surely I can expect no less before the Christmas tree." He drew her to him with a slowness that allowed time for the protest she never made. "One kiss," he said softly. "Just one. To do me a lifetime."

His lips were warm against hers. As his arms folded about her bringing her against him there was only a bittersweet ache for what was lost. Too soon he was drawing away, his hands framing her face in one last caress and then he was moving away. His broad back beneath the bright fabric of his shirt was staunch and erect as Christen watched, her fingers against her lips, keeping his kiss.

In the open doorway he turned, his eyes wandering over her, in their depth smoldered the desire he couldn't hide. A hard look crossed his face, as he struggled with himself. Then it was gone, replaced by an expression that was half sardonic, half regret. His lips curled in what was almost a smile. "You're a damn fine woman, Christen Laurence. You're batting fifty-fifty with the men in your life. One good one, one bastard. Maybe the next roll of the dice will bring the best yet. One bastard's enough for any woman."

The hard lines of his face eased. Softly he said, "The wrong time, Christen, the wrong place, the wrong world."

Then she was alone. Folding her hands tightly together to still their shaking, she looked about her deliberately, trying to see the room through Zachary's eyes. It was a nice room. No, it was better than that. It was lovely and gracious and filled with the treasures of Nathan's life. And for Christen, it was empty.

"Is this really where I belong?" Her whisper was the sound of tearing silk. The silent house gave back no answer. But, she wondered, what foolish question needed one? Her place had been decided.

Her step was heavy as she made her way from the room and up the winding steps to her room and her lonely bed.

The game was done.

The last of the February sun was warm on Christen's face. Only the barest nip in the air reminded that tomorrow would be the first of March and winter had yet three weeks to run its course. Beneath the terrace walls tiny flowers struggled through layer after layer of loam and leaves. In the meadows sweet smelling blooms with drooping bell-like heads were strewn in a haphazard garland through the first blush of green.

Only the smell of woodsmoke reminded that it was a changeling spring whose balmy days and crisp nights could turn in an instant to the furor of winter. But today, the last of February, was warm, and the sunlight could chase away the darkness of loneliness.

As if to tease her with its caprice, a cloud shrouded the sun, casting its chill shadow over the table where Christen sat. Tugging the collar of her jacket more closely about her, she glanced skyward. No storm gathered on the horizon. The weather would hold.

Even as she was turning back to the journal she was reading the sun was spilling over its pages. Bending to her task she read the same incomprehensible sentence she'd read a dozen times before. Medical diagnoses and suggested treatments were lost to her as subconsciously she waited for the thump of a tennis ball against a racket and a good-natured shout of disgust or of satisfaction.

She stared steadfastly at the book, but her mind was filled with visions of Zachary and Hunter, battling on the tennis court tucked out of the sight beyond the garden. With their rackets flashing they would range the court, moving with astonishing speed for men of their size. No quarter would be asked, none given. The winner would crow ungraciously, then both would dissolve into laughter with promises from the loser of "next time."

The days and weeks of the new year had flown by rather than crept as she expected. In them the bond between Hunter and Zachary had solidified and she was, as now, set apart, the observer. "It was the only way." Her spoken thought was lost in a distant flurry of shouts, but for once she didn't notice. Her pretense at reading abandoned, Christen's mind wandered as always to the evening in the library.

One kiss, he had whispered against her lips, a kiss to last a lifetime.

And then he had withdrawn from her and she from him. Though she grieved for the loss she knew it was the only way to ease the tension that lingered between them and diffuse the passion that threatened to erupt at any time.

"A penny." The journal slipped from her nerveless fingers, only Zachary's deft catch kept it from tumbling to the stone floor. "Sorry." He shrugged. "Didn't mean to startle you, but considering how deeply immersed you were in your thoughts, perhaps I bid too cheaply." He laid the journal aside and stood smiling down at her.

"A penny's too much for idle thoughts." Christen let herself look at him unreservedly for the first time in weeks. There was sweat on his brow, his hair was plastered in drenched curls to his face. The white shirt visible beneath the towel draped about his neck was transparent against his flesh. The golden pelt that swirled over the heavy musculature of his torso offered a marked contrast to permanently sun-bronzed skin and the puckered darkness of his male nipples. Drawn by their own will her eyes traveled the length of him, down the slim hips and glistening thighs and back again. Her breath caught, and embers blazed into flame.

As a breeze ruffled the pages of her journal and tousled the dampened gold of his hair she heard herself say, "Put on your jacket, Zachary." She gestured to the blue garment swinging carelessly over the crook of his arm. "Before you catch cold."

"Yes, ma'am," he said simply and she knew he understood more than her words expressed. The towel was thrown aside in favor of the more concealing cover of the jacket. Then he drew out a chair and paused expectantly. "May I?"

"Of course." She nodded with the regal calm of a duchess, then found herself at a loss for words.

"It's a beautiful day," Zachary ventured after he had settled himself with as much grace and comfort as he could on a chair not intended for one of his size. "Perfect for tennis, or for reading. Hunter sends his love."

"He's gone?"

Zachary nodded. "The bronze is ready for casting. He wanted to make a final inspection. Which is why he ran me like a jack rabbit over the court. Strenuous exercise to clear his head, he claimed."

"He beat you," she interpreted.

"To a pulp."

Christen laughed the obligatory laugh, hoping it did not sound forced. "I imagine you're evenly matched and the next game's scores could easily be reversed."

Zachary shrugged, deprecating his skills. "Hunter said you wield a mean racket."

"Hunter exaggerates."

"Does he?" The level blue eyes were fixed on her. In the sunlight the fine webbing about them crinkled into a grin. "Perhaps we could play? Speed versus strength. The beauty and the ugly."

Christen laughed. A real laugh that flowed like honey over him. "Even blinding speed would be no match for your strength." On an ill-advised impulse she touched his hand where it lay on the table before him, and immediately found her own trapped in his grasp.

"Why don't you like to be told you're beautiful?" The tone of his voice made her skin tingle.

"Because I'm not," Christen protested and felt the tingle become heat.

"You are." His fingers laced through her, his thumb tracing a mesmerizing pattern over the racing pulse of her wrist.

"Eye of the beholder," she said in an attempt at levity.

"And I am the beholder." His gaze held hers, saying things they'd promised not to say, offering pleasures that were forbidden.

"No!" Christen gasped and drew her hand from his grasp.

Anger, white-hot and sudden, glinted in his eyes. Not even the sweep of gold tipped lashes protected her from it. He drew a single breath, then released it. "Sorry," he said softly. "In my defense, you *are* beautiful."

"Thank you."

"For what? For the compliment or for the weeks of control wiped out by one jackass stunt?"

"For both." She waited for his look then offered a smile that was only a little tremulous around the edges. "And you aren't a jackass."

Zachary grunted, then smiled grimly himself. "Eye of the beholder."

"This time, that's me."

Overhead clouds drifted by the sun, bathing them first in brilliance then in shadow. An eagle soared in obvious delight in the day and Christen could only count each second that loomed like an eon in the nerve-racking silence.

"Have you seen..."

"How is..."

They spoke in unison, one as eager as the other to end the strain.

"Ladies first."

"Benjie," Christen faltered, nearly forgetting what she'd meant to ask. "How is Benjie?"

"He's well. The last tests were confirmed by Brighton. He's in remission."

"I've missed seeing him, but you've been good for him."

"No more than he has for me."

Christen nodded. Zachary knew. He was too astute not to have finally diagnosed his own ailment and, of course, he would recognize the change in himself.

"I've seen courage in the streets and on the battlefield but nothing like the courage of a brave little boy facing the unknown."

"Part of his courage comes from trust you've given him."

"Not enough to make him smile. What I wouldn't give to see him smile."

"You will." Perhaps she didn't think, or perhaps subconsciously she wanted to touch him and risk the bonfire she knew it would ignite. Whatever her reasons, her hand slid beneath his, her fingers folding about its sinuous strength as she murmured, "All things are possible if we dare to hope,"

"Are they?" His fingertips were like steel points burrowing into her flesh.

The telephone jangled, adding its own discordant command to the turbulence that engulfed them. Twice more it rang and after a pause twice more.

"I should get that," Christen murmured. "Bell's in the village."

"No!"

"It might be important."

"It could also be something as trivial as Lucy Foster in another drunken fit of hypochondria."

"It could also be about Benjie."

For the space of an angry heartbeat his fingers tightened over hers until she thought they would snap like brittle twigs. At her gasp he looked in astonishment as their entwined fingers, saw the cruel, punishing power he exerted. "Go!" he released her, his massive head shaking, his shoulders shuddering. When she hesitated his fist slammed onto the table. "Go, dammit! Before I hurt you more."

Christen rose, shocked by the violence she heard in him. Not because it was directed at her but because it was directed at himself. The telephone rang again.

"You'd better answer it." He was calmer now and oddly distant.

Her nod, a gesture of compliance, went unseen because Zachary was determined to look anywhere but at her. Feeling strangely defeated she went into the house.

Her footsteps were a dim echo before he rose and turned toward her. She wore jeans, her usual weekend attire, but as he watched the gentle sway of her walk he remembered the long, luscious length of a naked thigh. Sunlight in her hair became the gentle blaze of a dying fire. The secret bite of chill beneath the false February spring recalled long languorous hours of loving while falling snow turned their world into a crystal wonderland.

"Heaven help me, Christen, what am I doing to you?" He spun away. The force of his guilt taking him to the edge of the terrace. Returning from his game with Hunter he had glimpsed her here, sitting in the sun, a journal in her hand, her head bent over its pages. He had been drawn to her like a moth to flame. Telling himself all the while that just this once he could risk a quiet moment with her. He convinced himself he only wanted to listen to her voice and fill his lungs with her fragrance. He meant only to feast his hungry eyes on all that was lovely in her and never touch her, then she would be safe.

His hands gripped the rail. "She was safe, all right." His voice held the shattering roughness of a saw drawn over granite. "As safe as with a rutting stag."

No more, he promised. He would not hurt Christen or himself again.

"Zachary."

Returning for awhile from the private hell to which he consigned himself he found Christen at his side, her expression an odd mixture of joy and regret. When his look dropped to her hands she tucked them hurriedly behind her, but not before he saw the angry welts. Grasping her wrist he drew her hand forward seeing the hint of the bruises that would come. "This seems to be a habit with me."

"It doesn't matter. You didn't mean it." The hands with their offending marks were slipped again from his sight.

"There were a lot of things I didn't mean, but they happened. Forgive—"

"Zachary!" She cut short the apology she did not want. "The phone call, it was Nathan. He's well. He's coming home. He'll be here day after tomorrow."

He looked down into her happy face, into the glitter of emerald eyes that held a secret sadness. He and he alone had put the sadness there. "Two days," he said softly. Then this madness would end. "Enough time to pack and say my goodbyes and be out of your way before Nathan arrives."

"Surely you'll stay, to say hello if for no other reason."

"Another time," Zachary said grimly. "Now, if you'll excuse me, I have some calls to make."

"Of course," Christen murmured as he swept past her. Then slowly, with a heavy heart, she followed in his wake, going in search of Bell to tell her only the happy news.

Ten

Christen paused in her pacing, drawn by worry to a window that offered an unbroken view of a untraveled road and a lightless sky. How many times since Zachary came into her life had she roamed like this, sleepless and alone, through the darkness? How many lonely nights? she wondered. But none were as lonely as this.

It was Zachary's last night in Laurenceville, and he had vanished. After a day at the clinic filled with goodbyes he was simply not to be found. He sent no message. Bell delayed dinner until it was a travesty of overcooked foods for nonexistent appetites. Together they waited into the morning and still no Zachary. At last Bell had gone to her bed and only Christen waited in the silence.

A soft, hurting sound quivered in her throat. Her eyes burned from fatigue, as they searched for a car that never came. She shivered and, though the room was warm, drew her blouse more closely about her. The first warble of the library telephone did not register. As its sound penetrated her gloom she hurried to snatch it from its cradle, if perchance, Bell managed to sleep. The caller would be Lucy Foster with the latest Ben Casey symptoms, she decided, and was so sure of it the unfamiliar voice had to repeat its message. She listened a second time, in disbelief, to a tale of drinking and brawling in a cutthroat tavern.

"You're sure his name is Steele?" The receiver was slick with sudden perspiration. "He did! Can you keep him there?" She was reaching for her jacket as she spoke. "Do what it takes to hold him." The receiver clattered on the table. She was out the door before it tumbled to the floor.

Her skill at the wheel served her well. In less time than it should take, Christen was walking into a tavern that strongly resembled a battlefield. Chairs were broken and tables overturned. Its few patrons huddled in booths, speaking in subdued voices.

"Dr. Laurence."

Christen found herself looking into a face too lovely to be tending bar in this place. "Sally? You called about Dr. Steele? He did this?"

"I'm afraid he did."

"In heaven's name, why?"

Sally shrugged. "He'd been drinking. Something was said about his friend, the Indian artist. Called him a dummy or something. The doc didn't like it."

"Is he hurt?"

"Not as much as those calling names."

"There was more than one?"

"As a matter of fact there were three."

"Well, well, well," a familiar voice drawled. "The beautiful Dr. Laurence. 'scuse me. Forgot. She doesn't like to be called beautiful." He rose from a booth, swaying on his feet. "Sal, why wouldn't a woman like to be told she's beautiful?" He flung his arm about the blonde. "You don't mind if I tell you you're beautiful, do you?"

Hearing this sarcasm Sally's face clouded. "Should I have called you, Dr. Laurence? I didn't know anyone else."

"No," Christen said crisply, too relieved that his injuries appeared minor to take offense. "You were right to call. We don't always see eye to eye but I can handle him."

Zachary leered. "She can handle me all right. Like no other woman can."

"Sally doesn't want to hear our quarrel, Zachary." Hooking his arm about her neck she slid her own about his waist. "There's been enough fighting for one evening, let's go home."

"'zactly where I'm going tomorrow."

Christen did not answer as she walked him steadily toward the door. Sally was there before them. "Would you send me a bill for the damages, Sally?"

Sally nodded. "Doc, who's Benjie?"

Christen stopped, conscious of the weight of Zachary's arm about her and the brush of his hand against her breast with each breath she drew. "Benjie's a patient."

"Did he die?"

"No, but he's very ill."

"The doc kept muttering about Benjie and angels and smiles."

"It's a long story." Christen was beginning to make sense of this rampage.

"Yeah. Here, let me give you a hand."

With Sally's help Christen got Zachary into the truck. After a final thanks she engaged the engine and drove away.

Zachary was asleep immediately, his head resting on her shoulder.

He had not moved when she stopped before Nathan's house. In the light of a lamp burning in a window, she sat, reluctant to wake him, listening to the sound of his sleep. With her hand resting on his chest she found ease for her restlessness in the steady cadence of his heart. When the cold of March's many weathers began to creep into the truck she woke him. The patter of threatened rain was beginning on the windshield as she cajoled him into action. "Come on. We'll tend your wounds and then you can sleep it off." Sliding from the truck she guided his feet to the ground. "Tomorrow's hangover will exact a price of its own."

Half staggering, half walking, they made it into the house and up the stairs to Zachary's room where she lowered him to the edge of his bed and left him while she gathered first aid supplies and a basin of warm water. When she returned she surveyed the damage. His face was a livid mass of scratches and bruises but, miraculously, his mouth and chin were unscathed. "If you got the best of this deal, I'd hate to see the other guys. At least you don't need a dentist."

"They will," Zachary mumbled, speaking for the first time since leaving the tavern.

"Ahh, your tongue is working again, I see. So, why don't you tell me what brought on this carnage."

"Nothing."

"Nothing?" Her fingers were busy with the buttons of his shirt. When the task was finished she slipped it from his shoulder. Kneeling before him she probed red welts at his chest and the shadow of a bruise beginning over his ribs. His angel was missing.

"Ouch!" Zachary recoiled under her probing.

"No broken ribs," she said tersely, making no apology for the pain. Next she inspected his knuckles holding his wounded hands in her own. "You'll have a couple of sprained fingers for a few days, and these cuts on your knuckles will be slow to heal." She sat back on her heels glaring at him, hiding her relief that his injuries were minor. "I'm waiting to hear about the 'nothing' so important it caused a brawl."

"It was a rough tavern." The unfocused look was clearing. Zachary was rapidly sobering up.

"You'll get no argument on that." Christen dipped a cloth in the basin to bathe his face.

"Some fool insulted Hunter."

"I see." She shifted her attention to his battered right hand. "A right hook?"

"Several."

"Go on. Someone insulted Hunter?"

"An old schoolmate of Hunter's called him a dumb son of..." Zachary winced as she cleaned the deepest cut. "So I hit him."

"Accomplishing what?"

"Made me feel a helluva lot better, that's what."

"You could've played at being a doctor and explained about dyslexia, and that despite the fact he can't read Hunter's a very intelligent man. While you were at it you could've also explained that Bell is a fine *lady*."

"I didn't have time to explain. My fist got there first."

"Followed by his." The cloth was dipped again into the basin. This time her ministrations were to the livid marks over his ribs. Drawing the cloth across an ugly scratch she asked, "How long have you known about Hunter?"

"A while. Bits and pieces fell into place. The diagnosis was obvious." He gasped as she found a tender spot. "Dammit, Christen! I think you're enjoying this."

"What gave you that idea?" she asked sweetly. "This will sting," she warned and opened a bottle of antiseptic.

Except for a breathy whistle, Zachary sat woodenly. When the last scratch was painted he grumbled through hard bitten teeth, "It also rapidly produces a state of cold sobriety."

Christen made no comment as she packed away her supplies and rose, taking the basin to his bath. When the bloody water was discarded and the basin put away, she returned, pausing in the doorway to watch him. He sat stiffly. Despite his denials she knew his ribs hurt with each move.

In the unforgiving glare of her examining light his wounds were too vivid and raw. On impulse she snapped it off. Only a small lamp by his bed burned in the darkness. The half-light painted him in misty shadow, revealing far more than it obscured. With a breath of surprise Christen saw him as he might have been and as he was.

With medicinal color streaked garishly over his magnificent body, he was a man of many worlds. He was pagan, living by his wits and his heart, lashing out in his own anguish. He was Thor, golden god of thunder, wreaking havoc on any who hurt those he loved. He was a friend to Hunter and to Benjie. For them he battled cruelty and disease and his own despair. Zachary hurt, but his pain was more than a battered body.

Exasperated anger disappeared. Softly she asked, "Was it so hard to say goodbye to him?"

"Benjie?"

"That is where you disappeared to, isn't it? And why you went looking for trouble."

"No." He shook his head, then shrugged. "Yes."

"Did getting yourself knocked senseless help?"

Zachary lifted his head, listening to the rain. "At first he didn't understand that after today I wouldn't be a part of his life. When he did, he was afraid."

"Benjie has no concept of his illness, but he knows he's been better since you've been here," Christen said.

Zachary rose from the bed and crossed to the window. Rain slid down the pane like black tears. "What the hell have I done for him?" He asked in a low guttural whisper. "What *can* I do for him?"

"You taught him to trust." She made a sudden guess. "And left an angel to guard him."

His finger strayed to his neck where a chain had hung since his teens. "A piece of sentimental garbage."

"Not to you." She walked slowly to him, stopping an arm's length away. Close enough to stroke his tense shoulders, and brush golden hair from his face. Instead she clasped her hands before her. "She was your good luck. Maybe she'll be Benjie's."

His chest rose and fell. His hand dropped away from his chest. "When I put the chain about his neck he smiled. I was deserting him and he was afraid, and he smiled, Christen."

"I wasn't sure until this minute, but now I know Benjie will be all right." She touched him, laying her hands against his back, feeling the heat of his skin beneath her cool fingers. "You've done more for him than anyone else. You've given him a guardian angel and you've taught him to smile."

Like lightning Zachary spun around, catching her hands in his. There was still the bittersweet hurt of Benjie's smile in his eyes, but in those secret depths there were many things, a commingling of anger and pain, of fire and ice. "What have I taught you? Hate? Disgust?"

She slid her hands free of his, cupping one about his neck, the other covered his mouth. "I don't hate you. I couldn't."

"Not even for these?" His breath was like a furnace against her bruised fingers. He cooled them with his kiss.

Christen had bathed his bruises and tended his wounds. It was a part of her profession, but there was nothing professional about her need to draw his head to her breast and hold him until his heart eased. "I don't hate you, Zachary. Not for anything."

"Oh God! Sweetheart." He drew her to him, cradling her head against his chest. "What are we doing to each other?"

Christen pulled away. Not beyond the touch of his hands, but away from the strong enticement of his body. "We're saying goodbye. Tomorrow you return to your world."

"*My* world. *Your* world." He spoke in a low growl. "It has to be, doesn't it?"

She could only nod and look away.

His finger burrowed in her hair, lifting her gaze back to his. "Stay with me."

"Stay?" Her eyes shone like a winter pool at full moon.

"Just for tonight it could be *our* world."

Despair was a sudden hand about her throat. The leaping of her heart slowed to a dull throb. She wanted a lifetime, he offered an interlude. "We can't. Your face! Your ribs!"

He laughed, hugging her to him, holding her tightly to his aroused body. "You're so beautiful when you blush." The laughter that was a rare and wonderful sound faltered. "Stay, sweetheart," he whispered against her pulsing temple. "Let me love you."

She heard a desperateness in him. The disquiet of power leashed by tenderness, of deep-rooted sadness that reached one last time for the beauty of lost things. Lost. But not yet.

There was still tonight. Her face lifted from the bareness of his chest, her mouth seeking his even as he bent to her. Her answer was in her lips, her tongue, her caressing fingers.

Zachary guided her to the rumpled bed. At its edge her clothing and his were discarded slowly, deliberately, one revelation following another in a ritual of remembrance. Eyes feasted, lips met, tongues teased, reverent hands caressed. When the delicious task was done, he stepped away, the blue blaze of his eyes sliding over her. An emotion kin to rage seared him, setting his body to trembling. A part of him knew it as the unreasoning, primitive need of man to possess his woman. And she was his woman. From her tousled hair, shiny and bright as a new copper penny, to the creamy line of her throat, from the tawny-rose of her breasts to the shadowed secrets beyond, she was! If only for tonight.

"Christen." Her name was an endearment, his hand enfolding hers a caress. Tender and trembling he drew her down to his bed.

"Your ribs." She gasped as his lips found her breasts.

"Forget my damn ribs," he growled in a rasp that was fierce but not angry. "There are ways," he added gently as he lifted her, holding her poised above him, her hair tumbling over him in a river of silk. His body arched and was received by yielding velvet and her soft, wondering cry. "Dear God, yes," he muttered as her gentleness contained the furor of him. "There are ways."

Yes, Christen discovered. Wonderful, secret ways. Then the massive bed of dark, gleaming walnut became her world and she thought no more. With body and heart she learned the mysteries of a language more eloquent than words. The tide of passion rose, retreated into the quiet of spent ecstasy, and rose again. Time after time they were the sum of man and woman, of lust and love, until she heard her own anguished voice crying out. It was too beautiful, too exquisite to bear. Then her world exploded into a kaleidoscope of spangled light and sensation more beautiful, more exquisite. Anguish became joy, and joy had a name.

Zachary.

The sun was rising, its light a pale blush over tangled sheets and sweat-dampened bodies, when he drew her down to him for the last time. With his shoulder as her pillow, drowsy and pleasantly exhausted, she drifted into sleep to the melody of his whispered, "Sleep, love, sleep."

When she woke the sun was no longer a blush. In a cold glitter it fell over the coverlet in a broken pattern, looking like shards of glass. The bed was delicately carved out of cherry. The sheets were crisp and neatly tucked. My room, Christen thought. Forcing the cobwebs of sleep from her mind she leaned on one elbow. The move woke in her a deep throbbing that rose and fell like the ocean's tides in unison with the beat of her heart—the exquisite malaise, the pleasant pain of loving. Lying back, with one arm thrown over her eyes, she savored each tiny ache.

They had been simply Zachary and Christen, with no past, no future. Preordained paths were forsaken. Insurmountable differences did not exist. In the darkness of his room their hearts spoke. Finally, weary and unutterably happy, she had heard him call her love. Like a child she had curled against him, filling herself with the scent of him, feeling the heat of his flesh beneath her own, letting the steady rise and fall of his chest lull her deeper into contentment.

She dreamed of a golden Viking who whispered love. Not even Zachary's arms about her, or the sway of his walk as he'd carried her to her room disturbed her. Yet, deep in her subconscious, she remembered that a Viking more beautiful than a dream had drawn sheets that smelled of sunshine about her and whispered goodbye.

Christen was suddenly cold. The realist in her could no longer hide behind dreams. Zachary was gone.

Leaving the emptiness of her bed and slipping into a robe to cover her nakedness, she crossed to the window. Beyond it the valley lay bathed in evening sun. She had slept the day away. For a bitter moment she wished she could sleep her life away. But she was a survivor. Zachary had come back into her life as an enemy and gone as a friend. In that her life was richer.

Her melancholy thoughts were disrupted. What? Moving from the window she waited, her head tilted, listening. A flurry of voices rising in hushed excitement drifted up the stairs and down the hall. A boom of laughter followed, rich and deeply resonant. With the sound of it still ringing in her ears, Christen was out the door and down the hall, her feet barely touching the carpet. She flew down the stairs like she had wings. At the foot of the steps, she stopped, breathless, clinging to the banister, her heart pounding.

"Nathan." Her glittering gaze checked over him seeing the healthy shine of dark hair, the glow of strength beneath his tanned, trim body. The desert had worked wonders, he looked twenty years younger than seventy-seven.

Silently, as Bell watched from the doorway, Nathan opened his arms and gathered her into them. Holding her to him like a wounded child, he kissed her forehead and fiercely blinked back tears when she murmured, "I'm so glad you're home."

* * *

Christen strolled through the garden. The April evening was as unseasonably warm as those in February and March had been. Tender leaves seemed greener and flowers brighter as swollen buds burst early into bloom. The beds were raked and trimmed and what had been an untamed wilderness was again controlled exuberance. She knew of the many hours and hard labor needed to create the sense of naturalness. Few succeeded, but *this* garden thrived under a master hand.

"Nathan," Christen turned a worried look toward him as he knelt in the freshly turned soil of a bed that would be a lovely creation of ivy and lily of the valley spiked with multihued day-lilies. "Should you be doing that?"

"Honey, I've been back for two months and you've done nothing but fret over me." Nathan laid down his trowel and chose a bulb from a nearby basket.

"You're working too hard. We've been overrun at the clinic, and then you spend your evenings and weekends grubbing in the garden."

"This isn't work, child. It's a pleasure."

Christen recalled the months, before he'd left the mountain, when he hadn't the strength to work with his beloved flowers. "I know, but I wish you'd be careful. I wouldn't want to lose you again for months."

"I'm not going anywhere." Nathan watched her intently, seeing the weariness on her features. Christen was the one who drove herself. She worked too hard, her laugh was a little too quick, her calm too intense, too desperate. Rising with the restored energy of a much younger man, he went to her, holding her in his arms as if he feared she would shatter. He searched for words to express the regret that had lain on his heart for weeks. Finding there was no easy way, he said simply, "I'm sorry, Christen. If I'd only known about Zachary. About your past."

Christen listened to the strong beat of his heart beneath her ear as her own clenched in agony. "How could you know the one man you chose to fill your place was...was..."

"The only man you ever loved," he supplied.

"No!" Her denial was too urgent.

"Honey." He touched her cheek with a hand that smelled of flowers. "I've known since you returned from Brighton that a part of you would always belong beyond the mountains. We all knew."

"All? Even Greg?" Pain was closing about her chest like a vise.

"He knew better than the rest of us."

"I'm sorry." The tightness became a jagged thrust of remorse.

"Don't be. It was enough to know that the respect, yes, and the love, you felt for Greg was too great to offer him second best."

"I wanted to love him as more than a brother."

"He knew, Christen." Nathan stroked her hair as he had when she was a young girl discovering that love was not always as one wished it to be. "It made the hoping and the waiting worthwhile. He never regretted loving you."

"I wish—"

"Dear girl, wishes mean nothing to the gallant heart. It loves as it will, accepting no other." He smiled grimly at the aptness of his poetic phrase. His stroking ceased, his fingers tangled in strands of silk. "Have you heard from him?"

Christen didn't need to be told he spoke of Zachary. The entire subject, even when he spoke of Greg, had been Zachary. She suspected that what Nathan hadn't understood about her relationship with Zachary had been explained by Bell. "I won't hear from him. What was between us is finally resolved."

She drew away from him, certain he caught the subtle nuances of her words. Resolved, she said, not ended. What she felt for Zachary would never end.

"You could call. Just to speak to him. See how he is."

Christen shook her head. No words could be forced through the agony that convulsed her. To hide the sudden rush of tears she turned toward the setting sun hanging like a heavy ball over the blue misted mountains. She could not call Zachary. With his first word, her fragile pretenses would tumble into dust. Then, stripped of the last of her dignity, would she cry as she'd vowed she wouldn't? Would her body ache for him as it did each night in her lonely bed? Would she grovel then and would there be the same contempt in him as in her mother's lovers? She could bear anything but his contempt. Anything.

Nathan reached out to comfort her. His hand hovered over her shoulder, but never touched her. Realizing she had forgotten he was there, he withdrew his hand letting it fall limply at his side. Helplessly he watched the suffering she tried to hide. Quietly, regretfully, but with a burst of pride for her courage, he left her to brood in private in the fading light of the April sunset.

"I thought I would find you here."

"Have I become so predictable?" Christen smiled up at Nathan as he stood framed by the French doors that led to the terrace where she sat.

"This has become your favorite spot."

Christen laughed, a sound far less rare than it had once been. "I suppose it has."

Nathan heard a new contentment. The serenity in her level green gaze had pushed an innate sadness far into the background. "Are you certain you won't go to the Independence Day picnic? Bell prepared enough for an army."

"Thanks." She stretched languorously, her loose shirt draping the lines of her body. "I can see the fireworks from here. After that I think I'll get a little extra sleep."

"You're sure."

"Positive."

Nathan hesitated. A frown flitted over his face then cleared as he made a decision. "Christen." He moved closer.

Christen looked up. "Yes?"

He faltered in a rare moment of discomfort. "I don't know quite how to begin."

Only the tiniest ripple disturbed the serenity in her regard. She sat for a moment in utter stillness, then with a long, low sigh she murmured "You know, don't you?"

"That you're pregnant and the baby is Zachary Steele's? Yes, damn me to hell, I know."

"Don't blame yourself for this."

"I brought him here."

"And what I did, I did with my eyes open. I love Zachary and I grabbed the little of him I could have. I didn't plan the baby, but now that it's a reality, I'm not sorry."

"Is he happy about the child?" For the first time in weeks Nathan saw her calm fail her. She looked away, her eyes avoiding his like a scolded child. "You haven't told him."

"Not yet."

Nathan drew a chair forward and sat by her. With a finger beneath her chin he lifted her face to his. "He has a right to know."

"I don't intend to keep it from him."

"When will you tell him?"

"Soon."

"Will you call him?"

"I . . . No, I'm not quite brave enough for that."

"You promise it will be soon? You shouldn't face this alone."

"I don't want Zachary to feel trapped."

"Why don't you let him decide how he feels for himself?" Nathan patted her hand in his best grandfatherly fashion. "Would you like for me to stay home with you?"

"I think I'd like to be alone." She drew a pad and pencil from the stack of books that lay on the table. "I have a letter to write."

"If you need me. . . ."

"I'll know where to find you."

He leaned to kiss her forehead and rose to go. "Bell's waiting."

"Nathan." She waited until he faced her. "How long have you known about the baby?"

"Since April, when we talked in the garden."

Christen's eyes widened in astonishment. "I didn't know then myself."

"Bell knew. She saw it in your face. Who can explain it?" Nathan shrugged. "An Indian's instincts and woman's intuition are a formidable combination."

"Better than a physician's it would seem."

"Better than three of us. Tell him, Christen. Soon."

She sat listening to his retreating steps and the softly closing door. When the engine of the truck faded in the distance, she drew the pad closer, picked up her pen and began the most difficult letter she had ever written.

Impatiently Christen fished the keys to her truck from her purse. Three days had passed since the letter to Zachary had been mailed, and now the walls were closing in around her. "Bell, I promised Hunter I'd check on his house while he's in Houston."

"I was there this morning. Everything is as it should be."

"I think I'll check anyway."

"What about dinner? Nathan should be back from his house call soon, then you should eat and rest. You were at the clinic awfully late with Benjie today."

"Benjie's doing so well that seeing him is just a formality. It's a pleasure, not work."

"Just the same, you should . . . never mind. Go! I know you need space to think."

"There are times I think you're a mind reader."

"Humph," Bell grunted good-naturedly. "Doesn't require a mind reader to know the letter to Dr. Steele has been weighing on your mind. Shoo! One missed meal won't hurt you or the baby."

Once in the truck the anxiety that plagued Christen eased. The drive up the winding trail to Hunter's was almost leisurely. In the higher, thinner altitude, the lassitude that had enveloped her since the second month of her pregnancy wrapped itself around her like a fluffy cocoon. By the time she parked in Hunter's drive she was nearly asleep on her feet. "That's what three days with little sleep will do to you, pregnant lady." She scolded almost giddily.

She intended to spend the summer evening in Hunter's study reading, but found herself drawn to the edge of his lawn and the outcropping of rock that jutted over the precipice like the prow of a mighty ship. The view was very like the one from Sunset Ridge.

How appropriate, she thought, as she settled sleepily in the natural niche formed millions of years ago by a passing glacier. I'm watching a sunset from Hunter's lair, thinking of Sunset Ridge. Will my life be measured in days at the clinic and the sunsets that follow forever? The baby moved beneath her hand and she smiled, knowing that in five months sunsets would not be the measure of her life. The tiny butterfly flutter sent a drowsy thrill through her. The warm stone at her back and the July sun on her face seduced her. Her eyelids grew heavy, her weary body relaxed.

The crack of an acorn dropped by a startled squirrel woke her. The stone at her back was hard. The sun had cooled. She stretched leisurely, feeling the shirt pull across her thickening body. Languidly she opened her eyes and found Zachary crouched over her, staring fiercely at her.

"What the hell!" If his eyes were hot coals, his voice was the sound of the wind over a frozen tundra.

Christen's first instinct was to conceal her body from him, then she realized the gesture was far too late. "How long have you been here?" She managed to force her dry tongue to form the words.

"Long enough." His tone was thick with contempt. His icy-blue eyes plundered the length of her, from head to toe and returned to the swell at her middle. His face hardened even more, the eyes were colder. "The baby's mine."

"Of course."

"I'm not asking, lady. I'm staking a claim."

"You don't have to. I told you in the letter you could be a part of the baby's life or not. Your choice. It's not my intention to trap you."

"I don't know anything about any damn letter." He straightened, towering over her, his rage a violent throb at his temple.

"You didn't get my letter?" Christen's heart began a slow dancing beat.

"I told you I never—" He stopped, his eyes closed and in a shudder all the anger left him. His eyes opened and focused on her. Like a broken puppet he sank bonelessly beside her. Carefully as if every word required the utmost precision he said, "I've been camping out at the hospital. My house is too silent and lonely, and haunted by too many memories." He sighed wearily. "I never got your letter because I haven't checked my mail in days."

"Then why are you here?"

"Because I miss this place. I've discovered that flat land is boring. I missed the mountains and the valleys and Hunter and Bell and Nathan and Ginny and Benjie. I even missed Lucy Foster."

"You never met Lucy Foster."

"I missed her anyway. Hell, Christen, you know why I came back. I came for you."

"You came for me?" Disbelief warred with hope inside her.

"I got tired of looking at statues, pretending they were enough."

"Statues?" For a moment what he was saying seemed impossible. Then she understood—his unexpected knowledge of sculpture, the titles of works that rolled comfortably off his tongue, memories that haunted. Memories of her. "You're the mysterious collector who buys every piece of Hunter's work he can!"

"Not every piece." His voice was a low, rumbling growl. "Just the ones of you. And don't ask me why!"

She asked anyway, because she needed to hear the words. "Why, Zachary?"

"Because I love you, dammit." His hands framed her face, their gentleness belying the harshness of his tone. His laugh was humorless, self-mocking. "That wasn't exactly a romantic declaration, was it? My polish wears a little thin when I'm running scared. When you weren't at Nathan's I was petrified, afraid I wouldn't find you. I know it wasn't rational, but at the time, neither was I. It took a million promises that I wouldn't hurt you, before Bell relented and told me you were here. I wanted to hold you so badly, Hunter's mountain seemed a million miles away.

"Then I found you, lying against the stone in the light of sunset. You were so still, like one of Hunter's sculptures, distant, unreal. Then I saw your body and the child you carry, and I knew it was mine." His voice broke, his hands trembled. "My child. Mine! And you hadn't cared enough to tell me. I went a little crazy. I thought it meant you were running away from me again." A tear as lovely as a jewel, as precious, clung to his golden lashes. "Don't, sweetheart. Don't run from me. Not this time."

"I'm not running, Zachary." She had sat so still, not daring to move, now she turned her face into his palm, her lips caressing him. She was smiling a shimmering smile as she drew his hand over the fullness of her breast, holding it against her heart before bringing it to the baby. "Do you feel that?" She whispered, clasping his palm closely to her. "That's your son. He was conceived in love and if you'll let us, we'll go anywhere in the world with you."

"Let you!" Both hands molded her stomach, cradling the treasure she offered. His lips brushed hers, with the desperate gentleness of hunger barely contained. "Haven't you realized yet that I can't live without you?"

"You don't have to."

"Tell me." There was an underlying plea in the fierceness of his command.

"I love you, Zachary Steele. I have for years. I will forever."

Like the Viking she'd dreamed of he rose to his feet, swinging her into his arms. "Where?"

"The solarium," she gasped between his burning kisses. What better place than where he taught her joy?

The sun was slipping behind the mountain as he carried her over the lawn. Only the squirrels heard their murmured conversation.

"A boy?"

"Umm hum. Because of my age I had the appropriate tests."

"Some age."

"Zachary, where will we live?"

"Here. So Nathan can watch him grow up and Benjie can be his friend."

"He'll like that."

"Next time we'll have a girl."

"Next time?" she asked.

"Umm humm."

"Hadn't we better concentrate on our son first?"

"We'll call him Greg?"

"I love you," Christen whispered.

"Stop that, woman, or we won't make it to Hunter's solarium."

"Anywhere, but soon, and then I have a lot to tell you."

"You don't have to tell me anything."

"I do. About my mother and why I left you."

"Later."

"I forgot! Your sailing!"

"I'll learn to ski."

"But—"

"Dammit, Christen, will this shut you up?"

"Zachary!"

"Hush."

Silence descended over the lawn, after a time a squirrel ventured curiously from his hiding place and scampered away.

* * * * *

Now appearing
in a special return engagement, Nora Roberts's
bestselling 1988 miniseries featuring

THE O'HURLEYS!
Nora Roberts

Book 1   **THE LAST HONEST WOMAN**   *Abby's Story*
Book 2   **DANCE TO THE PIPER**   *Maddy's Story*
Book 3   **SKIN DEEP**   *Chantel's Story*

And making his debut in a brand-new title, a very special
leading man . . . Trace O'Hurley!

Book 4   **WITHOUT A TRACE**   *Trace's Tale*

In 1988, Nora Roberts introduced THE O'HURLEYS!—a close-knit
family of entertainers whose early travels spanned the country. The
beautiful triplet sisters and their mysterious brother each experience
the triumphant joy and passion only true love can bring, in four books
you will remember long after the last pages are turned.

Don't miss this captivating miniseries—a special collector's edition
available now wherever paperbacks are sold.

Double your reading pleasure this fall with two Award of Excellence titles written by two of your favorite authors.

Available in September

DUNCAN'S BRIDE
by Linda Howard
Silhouette Intimate Moments #349

Mail-order bride Madelyn Patterson was nothing like what Reese Duncan expected—and everything he needed.

Available in October

THE COWBOY'S LADY
by Debbie Macomber
Silhouette Special Edition #626

The Montana cowboy wanted a little lady at his beck and call—the "lady" in question saw things differently....

These titles have been selected to receive a special laurel—the Award of Excellence. Look for the distinctive emblem on the cover. It lets you know there's something truly wonderful inside!

You'll flip . . . your pages won't!
Read paperbacks *hands-free* with

Book Mate • I

The perfect "mate" for all your romance paperbacks

**Traveling • Vacationing • At Work • In Bed • Studying
• Cooking • Eating**

Perfect size for all standard paperbacks, this wonderful invention makes reading a pure pleasure! Ingenious design holds paperback books OPEN and FLAT so even wind can t ruffle pages – leaves your hands free to do other things. Reinforced, wipe-clean vinyl-covered holder flexes to let you turn pages without undoing the strap . . . supports paperbacks so well, they have the strength of hardcovers!

Pages turn WITHOUT opening the strap

SEE-THROUGH STRAP

Reinforced back stays flat

Built in bookmark

BOOK MARK

BACK COVER HOLDING STRIP

10 x 7¼ opened
Snaps closed for easy carrying too

Available now. Send your name, address, and zip code, along with a check or money order for just $5.95 + 75¢ for delivery (for a total of $6.70) payable to Reader Service to:

Reader Service
Bookmate Offer
3010 Walden Avenue
P.O. Box 1396
Buffalo, N.Y. 14269-1396

Offer not available in Canada
*New York residents add appropriate sales tax.

BM-GR